THE COUNTERFEIT MYSTERY

THE
COUNTERFEIT
MYSTERY

NORVIN PALLAS

WILDSIDE PRESS

To Elsie & Bob

CHAPTER 1

SUMMER DOLDRUMS

Rain, rain, and more rain. It had been raining steadily in Forestdale for nearly a week, just a light drizzle, not really hard enough to do anyone any good, but enough to interfere with most outdoor vacation pleasures. If it would only come down hard and get it over with—more than one person had been heard to grumble.

But now the rain seemed to have let up for at least a while, ushering in a cool but pleasant day, with a hazy sky in which the sun shone almost apologetically. Ted Wilford and his friend, Nelson Morgan, had taken advantage of the break in the weather to go for a swim, and now sat on the edge of the pool, basking in the sun and waiting to get up enough ambition to plunge once more into the cold water.

"Ready yet?" asked Nelson, not moving a muscle toward the water.

"In a minute." Ted, too, made no motion toward the pool. The park was located on the edge of town, and, being on slightly higher ground, gave a panoramic view of the community. Ted was in a meditative mood. These lazy summer days were fun but would soon end. A two-week vacation with his brother Ronald was coming up, and after that—college, and buckling down to a lot of hard work.

"Not a bad little town," Nelson commented, following his glance.

"No, I guess not," Ted agreed. "But I never really got to know any other town. I wonder how Forestdale will seem, after we've been away for nine months?"

"We'll be just aching to rush right back," Nelson predicted. "Why not? It's probably just as good as any other town, and it's familiar besides."

"You may be right. But so far we've lived here more or less because we had to. After college, I suppose we can sort of choose where we want to live. I wonder if we'll choose Forestdale?"

"Well, it's kind of a dead place at times," said Nelson critically, "but the newspaper manages to keep something stirred up most of the time. Mr. Dobson does his best to keep this the kind of town that's worth coming back to. What did you and Carl Allison argue about this time?"

Ted looked disgruntled. Having a close friend who could sometimes read your mind had its disadvantages.

"What makes you think we had an argument?" he demanded.

"Number one, you always do. Number two, you've been going around with your jaw hanging loose. Number three, you haven't gone near the *Town Crier* office for a few days."

"Well, I wouldn't exactly call it an argument," explained Ted carefully. "You know how things have been going down there. Mr. Dobson's still on crutches, and Miss Monroe hasn't been out of the hospital very long herself. I've been helping out wherever I could, but we've got the office work up pretty well. Then Mr. Dobson suggested to Carl that maybe *he* could use some help, and you would have thought the roof fell in. I don't mean Carl was rude to Mr. Dobson. He simply made it as clear as he could that he didn't need any help, and that just in case he did need any, I'd be about the last person he'd want for the job."

Nelson shook his head. "I'll never figure that guy out. He sure has got it in for you and Ronald. But you did manage to get along with him for a while, didn't you?"

"Sure, we got along as long as we had to. But sooner or later something always turns up, and we're back at swords' points again. Of course it *was* a silly suggestion. Carl doesn't need me, and Mr. Dobson was just trying to keep me busy. He must have thought Carl and I had smoothed things over while he was laid up. I rather get the impression Mr. Dobson feels Carl's still on probation. But Carl's been there nearly a year now, and Mr. Dobson'll have to make up his mind about him soon."

"And when he *does* make up his mind," said Nelson explosively, "he can give Carl a good boot out of there—with his *good* leg, I mean."

"And then what'll he do? He needs somebody. And Carl isn't the worst guy in the world, either. In fact, in some ways he's *good*. Just once in a while it seems to me he's not really enthusiastic about the newspaper business. I'm afraid he might pack up sometime and leave Mr. Dobson in the lurch."

"Well, that's Mr. Dobson's problem, not yours. Don't be crazy about it, Ted. Mr. Dobson doesn't expect you to give up college in case he finds himself short a reporter. You can just go off to college and forget the whole thing. You don't ever have to go near that office again, if you don't want to."

"Wrong there, Nel. I'm due at the office in"—he glanced at his waterproof wrist watch—"less than forty-five minutes. Mr. Dobson called me up this morning and asked me to drop in. He didn't tell me why, though."

Nelson showed interest. "Got something cooking again? I figured it was about time. Give Mm a couple of weeks back at the office, time to get things organized again, and then he's ready for another of his crusades. I hope it's something exciting. This deadness is getting me down." That was what Nelson *said,* but he looked as though having nothing to do but lie there the rest of the summer would be all right with him.

Ted got to his feet and flexed his arms. "As long as we came out to swim, I suppose we ought to get a little more swimming in. Coming?"

His friend did not reply at once. His eyes were fixed on the opposite end of the pool. Because of the early hour and the coolness of the day the pool was not crowded; even the lifeguard had not yet arrived. A group, chiefly girls, was gathered about the diving board. At its end a girl of about their own age stood gracefully poised—a summer visitor, they supposed, since they did not recognize her.

She raised her arms, gave two or three tentative bounces upon the board—and at that moment something happened. Apparently her foot slipped just as she was about to leap, and she flew off the board in a sprawling, awkward manner. Falling forward, she hit the water on her stomach, sending up a shower of spray. For a moment there was no sign of struggle.

"She's hurt!" Nelson was on his feet in an instant. The group standing about the diving board seemed immobilized, and there was no one else close at hand to offer help. Nelson dived into the water immediately, and swam toward the girl with powerful strokes.

Not quite so prompt to act, Ted sized up the situation in a moment, then ran around the edge of the pool until he was as close to the girl as he could get. Then he, too, dived off into the water. Although Nelson was the more skillful swimmer, Ted was able to reach the girl several precious seconds earlier. He grabbed her arm and helped her keep her head above water.

"You all right?" he asked anxiously.

"I—I guess so," she replied falteringly. "The fall kind of stunned me for an instant. But I guess I'll be all right in a minute."

"It's not far to the ladder," Ted encouraged her. "Think you can make it all right?"

She had nearly recovered both her breath and her self-possession. "I think so, but stay close beside me, will you? I'm not exactly sure."

They turned back toward the edge of the pool. The girl swam with determination, managed to make the ladder without any further assistance, and climbed up easily. Ted followed her up, and after them came the hapless Nelson, arriving just too late to be of any service.

An anxious group had gathered around the top of the ladder, and once assured that the girl was all right, began to joke about it.

"Where there's a damsel in distress, there's Ted!"

"I thought he was supposed to be working at the newspaper."

"Ken Kutler must have beaten him to a story, and they fired him."

"I'll bet he greased the diving board, Just to get a story for himself."

"My hero!" exclaimed a boy, one of a group who had just arrived in time to witness the outcome of the incident.

"And here comes our football captain, like the caboose on an empty train," another boy announced, as Nelson finally climbed the ladder.

"How about introducing us," someone suggested, "and finding out whether she's blonde, brunette, or redheaded?"

"I haven't introduced myself yet," said Ted, glad that a possible tragedy had been averted. The girl had withdrawn a little, not feeling herself a part of the group, but she waited and extended her hand as Ted approached.

"I'm very grateful to you. My name's Nancy."

"I'm Ted." Since she had given only her first name, he did the same. "And this is Nelson," he added, as his friend joined them.

"He's not always last. In fact, he won a medal for running fifty yards in ten seconds."

"A *hundred* yards." Nelson scowled at him, but smiled at Nancy as she acknowledged the introduction.

"You're a summer visitor, aren't you?" Ted resumed.

"Yes. That is, I *think* I am. What I mean is, visitor generally means being on a vacation, and I'm here to work. I'm doing secretarial work for my aunt, but we've had such a stretch of dreary weather she told me to take the morning off. I'm supposed to meet her for lunch, so I guess I may as well dress. I don't feel like doing any more diving."

"You don't want to lose your nerve," Nelson cautioned her.

"Oh, I don't think I've lost my nerve." She took off her bathing cap, and shook out her heavy, medium-brown curls, as though to show that she hadn't been much upset by the affair. "It's just that the fun's gone out of it for today, and I really do have to meet my aunt."

"Did you drive out?" asked Ted, realizing she must be alone, since no one else had joined her.

"No, I came by bus. I didn't have too much time, and I wasn't quite certain of the way."

It was unusual to take the intercity bus, though for a summer visitor it might be the most convenient way.

"Then why don't you let us drive you back, Nancy?"

"Oh, I wouldn't think of cutting your fun short. Go ahead and enjoy yourselves."

"You're not interfering. As a matter of fact, I'm due at work, too. Of course we haven't exactly been introduced—"

"But everyone here seems to know you, Ted, so I'm sure it must be all right, and I'd be very glad of the lift."

"It's Nelson's car, not mine, so I suppose I should have waited for him to invite you."

"Oh, don't mind me," Nelson grumbled. "You got to her first. It serves me right for leaping before I looked."

"But I think it was a very nice thing for you to try to help me, too," said Nancy warmly. "Swimmers sometimes get frantic, and it might have taken both of you. I appreciate it very much."

Nelson looked both embarrassed and pleased as he answered, "Well, we couldn't let you drown, could we?"

"I hope not!" She turned to Ted. "Where shall I meet you, then?"

"Right here. We'll be changing ourselves. See you in ten minutes?"

"Ten minutes," she agreed, and left them.

"Well, maybe I will, and maybe I won't," Nelson meditated, looking after her.

"Maybe you will or maybe you won't do what?"

"Write poison-pen letters to Margaret Lake."

"Oh, nuts!" Ted retorted, and started away.

Fifteen minutes later they were in Nelson's car and on their way to the business center of town.

"Are you going to be in town long, Nancy?" asked Ted.

"Only until school starts. I'm entering college this fall."

"So are we!" exclaimed Ted, unexpectedly pleased. Somehow, judging from her poise, he had thought Nancy to be a little older than they were, but now decided she was their age. That meant she might like to come along to certain social affairs that were likely to turn up soon.

They talked about college for a few minutes, which seemed to give them a common bond, even though the colleges were hundreds of miles apart. Nancy was interested in music, and Ted thought he might be able to find a place on the college newspaper or magazine. Since the conversation seemed to be leaving Nelson out, Ted mentioned that his friend had been a football star.

"Not this year," Nelson reminded him. "They don't allow freshmen on the varsity."

"But there'll probably be a freshman team—"

"Sure, a lot of work and no glory."

Though Nelson was driving slowly, Forestdale was only a small town, and they reached the center all too soon.

"Down this street—I think," Nancy directed them. "My office is along here somewhere."

"Mine, too," replied Ted. "Where did you say you worked?"

"Oh, there it is—that building next to the one with the yellow awnings."

"Why—that's the *Town Crier* office," exclaimed Ted. "I work there, too!"

Drawing the car to a stop, Nelson turned to them with a grin. "If you two work at the same place, maybe it's time you got acquainted with each other."

CHAPTER 2

BLUE HARVEST

It was a ridiculous situation, of course. The *Town Crier* had only three full-time employees in the office, Mr. Dobson, Miss Monroe, and Carl Allison, and that two people could work there even part time without knowing each other seemed incredible.

"You must be Nancy Lindell," Ted decided in wonder. "And Miss Monroe is your aunt. I've heard her mention you many times."

"Yes, and you must be Ted Wilford. She's mentioned you in some of her letters. I was hoping to meet you here, but didn't expect you'd be pulling me out of the water."

"But she didn't say anything to me about your coming here to work," Ted objected.

"No, it was a rather sudden decision. I wanted to come while she was ill, but I had another job, housekeeping for several children while the parents were traveling, and I couldn't get away. Anyway, I guess I wouldn't have been much good without someone to tell me what to do. Just the same, I was anxious to get in a little secretarial experience, so when she told me she could use me for a few weeks, I came right out."

"I haven't been down to the office since Monday morning," Ted explained, but did not add that his dispute with Carl Allison was responsible. "That's why I missed you."

They were feeling well acquainted already as they stood on the walk, Ted's hand still on the open door.

"I don't like to rush you people, but either I drop a dime in this parking meter, or else I have to go," Nelson finally remarked.

Nancy turned to him once more, and extended her hand. "Thanks, Nelson. I appreciate what you've done for me, and even more what you tried to do. I'm sure I'll be seeing you soon."

"You bet," Nelson agreed, and drove off whistling.

Holding open the office door, Ted followed Nancy in. Mr. Dobson was there, seemingly in conference with a man who was a stranger to Ted. But Miss Monroe was absent, which was only to be expected. There were always a great many things to be done outside the office, and as a normal thing work was arranged so that someone was in the office at all times. Now with Mr. Dobson's leg still not fully healed from the auto accident he had suffered at the beginning of summer, it was generally the editor who was there and his secretary who was out.

Both men looked up at the newcomers, and Mr. Dobson started to rise, momentarily forgetting his bad leg. Then he made a casual introduction, and Ted learned that the visitor's name was Mr. Woodring. They shook hands.

"I see you two have met," the editor observed to Ted, nodding toward Nancy. "Nancy, Miss Monroe said she'd be back before noon."

"That's all right. Perhaps she left some typing for me to do."

"And I can find something to help with," added Ted.

"Oh, no, no," Mr. Dobson objected. "I particularly asked you here, Ted, to meet Mr. Woodring. He has a proposition that I believe may be of some benefit to the whole town. Nancy, you might find it of interest, too."

Thus invited, the two young people drew up chairs.

"Mr. Woodring represents a trading-stamp company," continued Mr. Dobson. "He's told me a little about his plan, but I'll let him describe it again for you."

The visitor cleared his throat, hesitated a moment, as though not sure exactly how to begin—he wasn't quite so fluent as most salesmen are expected to be, Ted observed—then took out a folder from his sample case. He handed it to Mr. Dobson, who did not happen to have his reading glasses on, and so merely gave it a slight glance before handing it on to Nancy. She opened it and held it so that Ted could see, too.

It was a book of gummed trading stamps, called Blue Harvest stamps. Ted had never seen this particular kind before. They were beautifully tinted, and showed a rural scene, with a cow before a fence, cornstalks on the other side of the fence, and hills in the background.

"Pretty nifty," Ted decided.

"They are attractive," Nancy agreed, before finally closing the booklet and returning it to Mr. Woodring.

"I hear that Forestdale stores have been having a little trouble," Mr. Woodring began, "and I thought I might have the answer." He laughed. "Naturally, I'm concerned about my own interests, but if we're able to help each other out, then all the better."

"I've been telling Mr. Woodring something about the new shopping center in North Ridge," Mr. Dobson put in. "There can be no question that it is drawing trade away from Forestdale. Even some of our own townspeople are getting into the habit of driving over to North Ridge, and a great many of the country people living between the two towns seem to have developed a preference for North Ridge. Their stores are offering a larger stock at slightly lower prices, and that's a combination hard to beat."

"Why can't we match their prices?" asked Ted.

"I believe that's where I come in," Mr. Woodring continued. "It's largely a question of volume. If we could do something to stimulate local trade, volume would pick up, and lower prices would come. I frankly don't believe that there is enough difference to justify Forestdale people driving into North Ridge to shop. It seems to me they are going over now mostly as a matter of curiosity. My discount stamps would not only make up for the difference in price, but would also be a novelty that might induce them to come back."

"What do you think of it, Nancy?" asked Mr. Dobson, turning to her. "We're anxious to get the woman's point of view."

"I think it's a grand idea," said Nancy with enthusiasm. "We have trading stamps in my home town, and everybody seems to like them—anyway, the women do."

"And it's the women we have to consider chiefly," said Mr. Woodring quickly, "since they do most of the shopping. After all, you can't always get 3 percent on the money you *save,* so when you can get 3 percent on the money you *spend,* that looks like a pretty good bargain. The women are the ones who have to stretch the household budget. When they can earn valuable premiums they couldn't otherwise afford, it's easy to see why they like the idea."

He had another booklet in his hands which he handed to Nancy. It was filled with pictures of premiums, and Ted noticed at once an electric train and a number of familiar household items. This glance satisfied his own curiosity, since he did little shopping himself, but Nancy appeared much more interested, and continued to leaf through the book as the conversation went on.

Mr. Dobson seemed to be encouraging Ted to express an opinion, as though he wanted the plan to be thoroughly talked out.

"Who's paying for it?" asked Ted bluntly, determined not to be sold a bill of goods, but to try to find flaws in the plan if he could.

"Who's paying for what?" asked Mr. Woodring patiently.

"Well, for printing up the books and stamps and all. That's kind of expensive itself, isn't it?"

"Well, Ted, as far as that goes, we can be completely realistic about things. You know—and I know—that not all the stamps that are given to customers are going to be turned in. Some stamps are lost. Some customers start but never complete their books. My firm charges the stores for all the stamps we give them, but not all these stamps come back, and so we never have to redeem them. The difference is enough to cover the costs of keeping the plan moving."

"But who's paying for the premiums? Isn't it true that the customers are really paying for them, in the form of higher prices when they make their original purchases?"

"No, Ted, I don't think that's a fair way to look at it at all. A store sells merchandise at a certain price, as low a price as it can and still make a fair profit. Perhaps it would like to lower its prices to beat the competition, but it can't and still remain in business. Then a trading-stamp plan comes along. The trading stamps attract more customers, and because the store is doing a larger volume of business it can now afford to lower its prices. It appears to be charging the same prices, but its prices are really lower because the customers are getting these additional premiums. But no, I decidedly don't think it's fair to say the customer is merely paying for his premiums through higher prices. He'd have to pay these prices anyway. The plan is really being paid for by increased efficiency."

Of course he was a salesman for the trading-stamp firm, and he could hardly have been expected to express any other point of view. In fact, his company had probably trained him to make that little speech. Just the same, Ted felt that there was some sense in what he was saying.

"What I can't figure out is how *your* company makes any money," Ted maintained. "If you merely sell stamps to the stores, and afterward redeem these stamps from the customers, how do you make any profit? Just how does the Blue Harvest stamp company pay your salary?"

"I suppose, Ted, if you want to be blunt about it, the truth is that we're merchants, too. We're selling merchandise, the merchandise being the premiums offered in that book." He nodded toward Nancy. "You know that most stores buy their merchandise in large quantities, and because they buy these large quantities they are given discounts. They then sell to their customers at the full list price, and the difference between the two prices represents their margin. Out of this margin they have to meet all their expenses, and they hope to have a little left over for profit.

"Now my firm does about the same thing. We buy these premiums in large quantities, and get our discount. Then we sell to our customers at the full price. When a customer comes in to us with ten dollars' worth of stamps and selects a ten-dollar premium, that doesn't mean the premium cost *us* ten dollars. We bought it at a lower price. But that doesn't mean the customer is getting cheated, either," he added quickly, "for if he went out to buy that premium somewhere else, he'd have to pay ten dollars for it. The difference between the cost of the premiums to us and the price we sell them to our customers represents *our* margin, and that's what keeps us in business. Of course our customers don't pay us in cash. They pay us in stamps, but since we previously sold these stamps to the stores for cash, the result is the same."

"What if the North Ridge stores should adopt the plan, too?" Ted questioned. "Then wouldn't we be in the same predicament in relation to them that we are now?"

"That isn't likely to happen, Ted." Mr. Woodring's tone sounded wistful. "I don't say that we wouldn't like to have them adopt our plan, but they have a different style of operation. If they do adopt a trading-stamp plan, it won't be ours. But if the North Ridge stores do come up with some such plan, isn't that an even stronger reason why the Forestdale stores should have a plan of their own to meet the competition?"

Mr. Woodring had been addressing his remarks to Ted, but Mr. Dobson had been following closely, and it was to the editor that he now turned for a decision.

Mr. Dobson had evidently been giving the matter some careful thought, and he now seemed to have made up his mind.

"Yes, Mr. Woodring, you're right that our town *has* been having trouble keeping our sales up. Since North Ridge is a larger town, it may be that it does offer attractions to buyers that we can't hope to meet but we should at least be able to hold our own, and it may be that your trading-stamp plan will do it. At least, I think it's worth a trial."

Mr. Woodring rose to extend his hand to the editor. "Thanks. I've heard something about your reputation, and how you get behind local projects, so I was hoping I could interest you."

"But it's still up to you to sell the plan to the merchants," the editor cautioned him. "If you can do that, the newspaper will stand behind you with publicity and an advertising plan such as we were discussing before Ted and Nancy came in."

Having made his sale, a good salesman leaves promptly, and Mr. Woodring was about to do so when he added:

"By the way, now that you've accepted my plan, I feel I'd better go ahead and open up some office space. Do you know of any place that happens to be vacant?"

"There's the Jackson Realty Company office on Poplar Street," Ted spoke up. "They moved out a couple of weeks ago, and I noticed this morning it's still vacant. Of course I don't know whether they've got a new tenant lined up, and it isn't very large."

"That sounds like it might do," said Mr. Woodring quickly. "I don't need much space—just a desk and a telephone and display room for some of my premiums. I may need it for only a few weeks. Sometimes my firm opens up a permanent premium store, but I don't think the volume will justify it in this town. Later, people will have to order their premiums by mail. But just now I think I ought to have some display space. It might help arouse a little customer interest and curiosity, if nothing more. Incidentally, you needn't regard anything I've said today as being at all confidential. The more publicity you can give to the plan the better."

He said good-by to each of them by name, picked up his brief case into which he had stuffed his exhibits, and opened the door, almost bumping into Miss Monroe, who was just returning. Pausing only to excuse himself, he hurried on outside, and was soon out of sight.

Miss Monroe seemed pleased that Ted and Nancy had become acquainted. Nancy hurriedly described her meeting with Ted at the swimming pool, but while she wanted to give Ted full credit, she made light of her own fears. Ted, too, followed her lead.

"She could have made it all right by herself," he joked, "but it was more fun this way."

"Well, what about lunch?" asked Miss Monroe, laying down her notebook and purse on the desk as though she had had a frustrating morning. "Will you join us, Mr. Dobson?"

"No," he returned with a smile, but still thoughtful, "I'll stay here and tend to the shop until you get back."

"How about you, Ted?" asked the secretary.

Having lunch with Nancy would have been fun, but Ted declined. There was still a question in the back of his mind. This Blue Harvest plan was interesting enough, but where did *he* fit in? Mr. Dobson had asked him to sit in on the conference, but for what purpose? It was hardly just a courtesy. After all, Mr. Dobson didn't owe him any favors, although for some reason he seemed to think he did. Ted had an idea that Mr. Dobson was waiting to get him alone before broaching some sort of proposition.

"I'd like to very much," he answered, "but I'm expected home for lunch"—which was the truth. "Anyway, I hope I'll be seeing you again soon, Nancy."

"I hope so, too, Ted," she returned with a smile as she and her aunt left the office.

CHAPTER 3

HUMAN NATURE

When they were alone, Ted sat down in the chair near Mr. Dobson's desk. As he had surmised, the editor had indeed wanted to talk to him, but took time to light up his pipe before proceeding to business.

"Ted, Mr. Woodring is going to need someone in his office, someone to answer the phone and handle inquiries while he's out—and he expects to be on the road a good deal. I told him I'd let him know if I could find anyone, but I had you in mind. He mentioned something about it when I spoke to him on the phone early this morning, which was the reason for my call to you. It wouldn't be hard work, and you might even find it dull, since you'd be sitting around alone most of the time. I certainly don't want to interfere with any plans you may have for yourself, but it would probably be for only a few weeks, and the job is yours if you want it."

Ted hesitated. He didn't mind taking the job, even though it did seem a little dull, for it would give him something profitable to do during the next few weeks. But first he had to be sure it really was a useful job, not just some made-up work Mr. Dobson had devised out of a feeling of obligation to him.

"Are you sure he really needs somebody?" he asked.

"Oh, yes, he honestly does, and if you don't take it I'll try to get someone else for him. I may as well make it clear to you that if you start the job, it will be the newspaper and not Mr. Woodring who is paying your salary. This will be part of the help I promised him, in case he's successful in interesting merchants in his plan. Of course our interest is clear. Anything that helps our merchants helps our advertising. That's being a little crass about it, since my principal desire is to do something which I feel is good for the whole town, but it would be hypocritical to deny that we have a self-interest in the plan, too."

"I guess I'll take the job, then, if he really wants me," Ted answered, but couldn't avoid a feeling of disappointment. When Mr. Dobson had phoned him that morning, Ted had been led to hope that something big and exciting was in the wind. Well, life wasn't always like that. A thing could be big and important, but not very exciting.

Mr. Dobson swung about in his swivel chair until he was directly facing Ted. "I've one little point to make, Ted, and I certainly hope you won't misunderstand me. I first had an inquiry from the Blue Harvest people a few weeks ago. Naturally, I checked their references, and I find that while they are a new company, the investors behind the firm are persons of integrity. I then replied, expressing interest, with the result that Mr. Woodring was sent out to discuss the matter. Now I've nothing against new companies, but at the same time they often make mistakes due to their inexperience. They may have a slipshod sort of organization, they may make promises that they later find themselves unable to keep.

"I'm sure you'll understand that I'm not asking you to spy on Mr. Woodring. But he knows that you're working for the newspaper, and that you will be reporting back to me from time to time. He's presented a plan which I've accepted in good faith, and so I don't think it's wrong to suggest that he preserve good faith with me. If anything should come up—anything at all—that suggests his plan of operation isn't exactly the way he presented it to me, then I expect you to have no hesitancy in telling me about it."

This was growing a little queer, Ted thought. If Mr. Dobson had any doubts about the scheme, why did he let the newspaper get tied up with it? But maybe this was nothing more than his natural caution in dealing with a new company and with people who were strangers to him. After all, he had spent decades building up the newspaper's reputation in the community and couldn't afford to let anything happen to that reputation.

"Do you know anything about Mr. Woodring?" Ted inquired. "He seemed like a good sort to me, and it looks like he knows his onions. He was ready with an answer for anything we could say."

Once more the editor hesitated. "Yes, Ted, I'm inclined to agree with you. But I must admit there was one small thing that came up while I was talking with him earlier. I don't recall just how it came about, but he said he'd worked for the firm of Beacon, Jones and

Western in Chicago, about ten years ago. Of course he had no way of knowing that I know anything about the company, but it happens that I do. And the fact is that there wasn't any firm called Beacon, Jones and Western ten years ago. Beacon and Jones only merged with Western about five years ago."

Ted considered, but was obliged to conclude that this wasn't a very serious breech. "If he worked for Beacon and Jones ten years ago, it would be only natural to give the present name of the company instead of the old name, wouldn't it?"

"Yes, perhaps. Oh, yes, certainly it would. However, this does give me a chance to check up on Mr. Woodring. I know someone at Beacon, Jones and Western who has been with them for many years and would be in a position to consult the personnel records just to make sure Mr. Woodring really was employed there at that time. The whole thing would be on a strictly confidential basis, and if it turns out that everything is just as Mr. Woodring said, then there's no harm done."

Once again Ted thought Mr. Dobson was being excessively cautious. But he reflected there was certainly nothing wrong in what the editor was proposing. When someone presents a business proposition which demands a high degree of confidence, he can expect that some inquiries will be made about his background.

"I'll call Mr. Woodring, then," said Ted, rising. "Did he leave a number with you?"

"He's staying at the hotel. You should be able to reach him there."

Since Forestdale boasted only one hotel, Ted had no trouble putting through the call shortly after he had had his lunch at home. Mr. Woodring was out at the time, but Ted left his number with the desk clerk and asked Mr. Woodring to call him back.

Shortly afterward Nelson phoned, eager to hear what Mr. Dobson had had to propose. When Ted explained briefly about the Blue Harvest stamps, Nelson groaned.

"Is that all? I thought he was all ready to come up with some nice, juicy political scandal, or at least something controversial that'd have everybody taking sides and arguing. I thought there'd be something to stir up this dead town, and now it's only some moldy old stamps. Holy cow!"

Ted could imagine Nelson's expression, and he laughed.

"What's the matter?" Nelson demanded. "Did I say something funny?"

"Not intentionally. But it happens that these stamps do have a picture of a cow on them."

"That does it," said Nelson with a deep sigh. "Well, I suppose it'll work out all right. Women always fall for these phony schemes."

"What do you mean, phony?" Ted retorted. "Mr. Dobson wouldn't be mixed up in anything crooked."

"I didn't say it was crooked," Nelson explained. "I just said it was phony. Look, I stopped believing in Santa Claus when I was five years old, but some people still think they can get something for nothing. It's human nature, I suppose."

"Well, they do have their budgets to watch out for," Ted returned. "And as Mr. Woodring explained it, the plan helps the stores sell more efficiently and the saving is passed on to the buyers."

"Sure, the old, old game, something for nothing. Efficient? That's only because they don't count all the extra work. Buyers have to sort out their stamps and paste them in their books and get them redeemed, but they don't get paid for any of that. Well, you'll never catch *me* fooling around with those things."

Ted laughed. "Why do we have to worry about it? Merchants are pretty shrewd, and if the stamps help business they'll keep on with them. Otherwise they'll drop them. It's a problem that'll solve itself."

"O.K.," Nelson agreed disinterestedly. "What's for tomorrow, Ted? How about a drive out to the lake and—"

"Nothing doing, boy. I've got a job now. Mr. Woodring needs some office help for a couple of weeks, and I'm elected."

"Well, there goes the rest of our summer up in smoke. How'd you make out with Nancy?"

"All right, I guess. I'll be reporting to Mr. Dobson off and on, so I suppose I'll be seeing more of her."

"Lucky dog. Now I know why you wanted to work." And Nelson hung up.

They hadn't talked very long, and Ted hoped Mr. Woodring hadn't called and found the line busy. But it soon appeared that he hadn't, as the hours dragged on and no call came. If Ted were going to work tomorrow, there were several little matters he wanted to take care of, but he felt bound to the telephone. He picked up a book and tried to read, but his mind was on other things as he found himself half-listening for the phone.

It was late afternoon when the call came. Mr. Woodring was brisk and businesslike.

"Ted? I got your message. I'm sorry that I was out, and only got back a few minutes ago."

Although he must have known why Ted called, he took nothing for granted, and waited for Ted to state his business.

"Mr. Dobson tells me you're in need of office help for a few weeks, and I thought maybe I could fill the bill. I'm looking for something to do, until I leave town in about three weeks. Mr. Dobson said you probably wouldn't need me for longer than that, anyway."

"That would suit me just fine, Ted. I managed to rent that office you spoke of, and the phone will be in early in the morning. How soon can you report for work?"

"Tomorrow morning would be all right with me."

"That's fine. I'll see you at nine o'clock, then. Good-by." And the conversation ended as abruptly as it had begun.

Ted decided he would have time for a quick trip downtown before supper, and left almost at once. He had library books to return, and a few purchases to make, and he stopped in front of the theater just to see what would be playing during the next week. There was a horror picture coming, and he didn't feel that would do, for he doubted that Nancy would care for that kind of picture. Suddenly he wondered what had made him think of Nancy just then.

When he arrived home he told his mother about his new job and asked her for her opinion of the trading stamps. She wasn't likely to be carried away by fads or something-for-nothing schemes.

"It sounds like a good idea to me, Ted," she decided. "Women seem to like that sort of thing. It's sort of like a saving plan. You want something that you really can't afford, so you save up until you can afford it."

If his mother liked it, Ted decided that most of the other women would, too. In a way he was glad, even though he couldn't work up a whole lot of enthusiasm for the plan himself. He wouldn't have wanted to see Mr. Dobson betting on a dead horse.

Later that evening the telephone rang again.

"It's for you, Ted," his mother called to him. "Nancy Lindell."

Ted was momentarily pleased, but then surprised and puzzled. Why was Nancy calling him? It wasn't likely she would call a boy she just met that day, unless it was about something pretty important.

"Hello, Nancy?" he answered.

"Ted, I've got to know something right away." Her voice sounded troubled.

"Go ahead, Nancy," he urged her, as she paused.

"Ted, did I take your job away from you?"

"Why, no, Nancy," he said in surprise. "What makes you think you did?"

She seemed relieved, although not fully convinced. "Well, Ted, you used to come into the newspaper office almost every day, didn't you? And now I've just heard from Aunt Marian that you're going to start working for Mr. Woodring. I did take your place, didn't I?"

"Oh, no, you didn't, Nancy. You mustn't think that. Of course I came in every day while they were shorthanded, but that's all over now."

"But if I weren't here, you'd still be coming in, wouldn't you?" she persisted.

Ted remembered his long months of feuding with Carl Allison but couldn't bring himself to explain. "No, Nancy, I honestly don't think so. Besides, you're not even doing the kind of work I was doing. I had very little to do with the filing or the correspondence. I don't even know shorthand."

"Well, I hope you're not just saying that to be polite, Ted, because I'd feel awfully bad if I thought I really was interfering. It isn't that I have to work, but I am glad of the chance to get some practical experience, and Aunt Marian seems to like to have me around. However, I'd quit in a minute if I thought it was hurting you."

"Not at all, Nancy, not at all," he said quickly. "I think I'm going to like my new job. It'll be a change, and even if I don't like it, it's only for a few weeks anyway." The truth was that he was still working for the newspaper, over at Mr. Woodring's place, but he decided not to mention that. If Mr. Dobson wanted it known, he could tell her.

"I hope you do, Ted. It does help to get around into different places, doesn't it? I feel I've learned a whole lot in just the few days I've been at the newspaper."

Ted thought quickly about that movie again. It was the only movie in town, and he didn't have a car to take her to North Ridge. He couldn't ask a girl like Nancy to go to a horror movie like that—or could he?

"Nancy, I was going to ask you to go to the movies Saturday night, but it's about one of those monsters from outer space—"

"Why, Ted, that's just what I love! I always like to see if I can get scared, but most of them are too tame."

Ted brightened. "Then would you—could we—"

"Sure, Ted. Saturday night. Aunt Marian's waiting for me, so I'd better hang up. Good-by now."

Reluctantly Ted replaced the receiver.

CHAPTER 4

AN UNPLEASANT DISCOVERY

At a quarter to nine Ted was waiting in front of the new office. He thought it would make a little better impression to arrive ahead of time the first day, but he had to wait just fifteen minutes, for Mr. Woodring arrived precisely on time.

"Good morning, Ted," he said briskly.

"Good morning, Mr. Woodring," Ted responded, but his new boss had already turned away and was unlocking the door. It was quite a small office and at the moment a desk, a chair, a wastebasket, and an empty coat rack were the only furnishings.

"The phone will be in soon, and I've already given the number to some interested prospects, so there may be some calls."

"What shall I tell anyone who calls?" Ted questioned.

"Well, in the first place, it will probably be people who will want an appointment with me. I have my appointment book here." Mr. Woodring drew it from his brief case and laid it out flat on the desk. "Now you can see that on certain mornings and afternoons I'll be out of town and won't be available for local appointments. I try to avoid being absent for a whole day at a time if I can. If the caller asks for an appointment, you can look at my schedule and see when I'll be available, and make an appointment for me."

"What if they only want some information?" asked Ted.

"Then give it to them, of course, if you can. Don't try to answer if you aren't sure, but just tell them they'll have to get in touch with me. Still, I'd much rather have you try to steer them into making an appointment. That will give me an opportunity to outline my whole proposition to them and perhaps cement the deal."

"But if all they want is information, I'm not sure I know enough about this to tell them," Ted objected.

"There isn't a whole lot to tell. You're familiar in a general way with how the stamp plan works, aren't you?" Ted nodded. "I've got samples of my supplies available for anyone who wants them, and I'll put a few of each in the desk. But don't try to answer any questions about money, or anything like that. It would be too complicated, and I'd have to go into it myself."

"Then all you want me to do is answer the phone?" asked Ted, disappointed. He didn't think there would be very many calls, at least not today, and he saw a long, empty day stretching out ahead of him.

"There's one other thing," Mr. Woodring suggested. "You may get an express shipment this morning. I had it addressed to the hotel, since I didn't know just where I would be opening an office, but I left word there to have it transferred over here. The shipment consists of premiums which we are offering for stamps when they are redeemed. You can open the packages, and then arrange a little display in front of the window. That may arouse the curiosity of passers-by, and if they come in and ask a few questions about the stamps, that will be all to the good. I've got some posters here, too, which you can put into the window, but don't put them up until the shipment arrives. There wouldn't be any point in having people come in before we've got something to show them. The posters will tell people what's going on. I don't believe it will be worth while to put any lettering on the door or window for the few weeks we'll be here. Everything clear?"

"Yes, I think so," Ted agreed. It surely didn't sound very complicated.

"Fine. I'm leaving now, and I'll be back again at three o'clock."

He picked up his brief case, and with an abrupt nod of his head left the office.

Being alone in a business office would have given Ted a feeling of being in charge of things, except that there wasn't very much to take charge of. There wasn't even a typewriter, and all the drawers of the desk except the top one were empty, as he discovered after a quick investigation. Ted wondered what he ought to do. The place didn't look very presentable and could very well use a sweeping out. In a back closet Ted found a broom and dustpan, among other odds and ends, and went to work, raising a little cloud of dust. When that was finished, he dusted off the desk and chair and returned the utensils to the closet. The window was perfectly clean and bright, and so there seemed nothing more for him to do.

He hadn't brought a book or magazine with him and considered ducking out for a minute to pick up something to read from the corner drugstore, but decided against it. If someone came in and found him reading, it would look as though they didn't have very much business—which, alas, was the truth.

No, the best thing to do was to look busy, and he decided he could begin by looking through the samples Mr. Woodring had left. This would at least make him more familiar with their line, and perhaps he could answer questions more intelligently. He was about to start when the telephone man arrived, and for half an hour there was too much interference to allow him to settle back in his chair.

"That'll do it," the installation man finally announced, and Ted thanked him. At least having a telephone offered the possibility of something doing.

More dust had arisen in the process, and Ted swept out the office once more. Then he settled back to look over his material. There were a number of empty stamp books on hand—but no stamps. Apparently Mr. Woodring hadn't wanted to leave any of these lying around. If anyone wanted to know what the stamps looked like, he could find out from the large illustrated posters which were later going to be placed in the window. They showed an enlarged stamp, of the same design Ted had seen the day before, except that the picture looked even more attractive. The details stood out more vividly than they did when the illustration was reduced to less than the size of a postage stamp.

The catalogue showing the premiums to be earned was next to receive Ted's attention. He ran through it briefly, admiring some of the items shown, and then was distracted by the arrival of an express truck pulling up in front.

There were about a dozen parcels altogether, which was more than Ted had expected, and he helped the expressman carry them in. The largest could be nothing except a bicycle, but Ted had no idea what the others were, and looked forward to opening the packages. After he had signed for the delivery, and the expressman had left, Ted used his pocketknife to cut the stout cords and rip carefully through the wrappings.

He unveiled the bicycle first, and was agreeably surprised. He had seen it pictured in the catalogue, but pictures often look more beautiful than the real thing. This bicycle looked just as fine as the picture, which was saying something. Any boy, including Ted himself if he had been younger, would have been proud and delighted with it.

He began to open the other packages. There was a beautiful doll, elaborately dressed, which would certainly have warmed the heart of any small girl. And there was a portable radio—just the thing for picnics—and a number of household utensils. Whatever reservations Ted had about the stamp plan, he had to admit there was nothing shoddy about these premiums. It was all first-class stuff.

All the wrappings lying on the floor made a pile too large to be fitted in the wastebasket, and Ted carried the trash out the back door and deposited it in a can. Then he was ready to organize his display. The smaller items could be placed in the window, and he arranged them as tastefully as he could. The bicycle, of course, was too large for that, but Ted stood it just behind the window display, where he knew it would be clearly visible from the street. And the posters— Ted found a roll of sticky tape and hung one of them in the window. The other he decided to hang on the office wall, where it would be readily seen by persons coming into the office.

Finally Ted had to sweep out the office for the third time, thinking meanwhile he might end up by joining the janitors' union. Before he had returned the broom to the closet again, the telephone rang. The caller did not offer to give his name, and refused to make an appointment, although Ted suggested it as strongly as he felt he could. Instead, the man left a number where Mr. Woodring could reach him, and hung up.

Then a few of Ted's friends happened by, saw him there, and dropped in to see what the score was. They didn't stay very long, however, and Ted didn't encourage them to hang around. They inquired a little about the stamp plan, looked over the premiums, then suddenly remembered it was almost time for lunch.

"Don't make any dates for a week from Saturday night, Ted," Cliff Corby called over his shoulder as they left.

"Why not? What's coming off?"

"Don't know yet. Remember when we took the girls roller skating a couple of weeks ago they said they were planning something in return? They won't tell us what it is."

Ted was mildly curious, and glad that there would be another get-together soon. He suddenly realized the summer was going fast, and there wasn't much time before the fall college season set in. He wondered if he could get Nancy included in the affair. He felt he ought to do something to help her get acquainted in Forestdale, but he didn't know just how he could work it, as long as the girls were planning the party.

And then the noon whistles began to blow, and Ted wondered what he ought to do for lunch. He hadn't planned on going home. But while he could easily drop in to a nearby restaurant, he suddenly remembered he didn't have a key to the front door, and he hated to leave the place open and deserted. The back door could be bolted, he discovered, and he decided to eat at a drugstore across the street, where he could keep an eye on the front door.

Better go now, Ted thought, for very likely Mr. Woodring would call in after lunch, and he'd want to be sure and be back. He went out across the street and into the drugstore. He ate slowly, and found it rather pleasant to watch across the street, where a number of passers-by stopped to gaze curiously into the window. At least Mr. Woodring was getting a little bit of publicity for his stamp plan.

After finishing his lunch, Ted would have liked to take a little walk, but he still didn't care to get out of sight of that open door, so he merely took a short stroll up the street.

Shortly after one Mr. Woodring did call, long distance, from a nearby town.

"Any messages, Ted?" he asked.

"Just one call. Somebody left a number and wants you to call back."

Ted gave the number, and Mr. Woodring apparently wrote it down. "Is that all?" he asked, and his voice sounded disappointed.

"Yes, I guess so," Ted replied, and tried to sound a little more cheerful. "Maybe people don't know we've got a telephone yet."

"Well, maybe."

"The premiums arrived, and I've made up a window display."

"Good. How do you like them?"

"Fine. They're good-quality stuff."

Mr. Woodring's voice suddenly became brisk. "I'll be back before four o'clock then, Ted, unless this appointment delays me. If I should be late, you can just pack up and go home anyway."

"You didn't leave me a key," Ted reminded him.

"Oh, that's right. I forgot about it. Well, anyway, I'll be there before closing time. There's no use putting in any overtime with the little business we've got." His voice sounded rather bitter once more, as though his morning calls hadn't gone over too well. "Good-by, Ted."

"Good-by, Mr. Woodring," and they hung up.

Once more the office was still, the passing traffic hardly disturbing the calm. It looked like a long, dull afternoon ahead. Ted recalled that he had started to glance through the catalogue and been interrupted several times. Well, this time he'd really get at it. Yes, the premiums were attractive, and the bicycle especially got him. He began to wonder how long it would take the average family to earn a premium like that. Maybe it would be so long that the boy in the family would be grown up before he could earn it! He looked to see what the catalogue had to say about it. Thirty books! Then he saw there was an alternative in smaller type. The bicycle could also be obtained for five books plus seventy-five dollars. Wow! It was a wonderful bicycle, of course, but the first way would take an impossibly long time, and the other would take a fairly substantial cash outlay.

How much was each book worth, then? Well, that was very easily figured out. You could work it as an algebra problem:

$$30x = 5x + 75$$
$$25x = 75$$
$$x = 3$$

Or to put it another way:

$$30 \text{ books} = 5 \text{ books plus } \$75$$
$$\text{subtract } 5 \text{ books} = 5 \text{ books}$$
$$25 \text{ books} = \$75$$
$$1 \text{ book} = \$3$$

Three dollars a book—that sounded about right. Ted remembered that Mr. Woodring had spoken of the plan as representing a 3 percent saving. Just to make sure he worked it out for a mechanical toaster, and it came out the same. On some of the smaller premiums it wasn't possible to make such a calculation, because the premiums could be obtained only for stamps. The doll, for example, was listed as five books. That seemed all right to Ted. It looked like a fifteen-dollar doll, as far as he could tell.

That meant that a family would have to spend a hundred dollars in order to fill a book and earn three dollars toward a premium. The bicycle, then, costing thirty books, would mean that a family would have to spend three thousand dollars! That was a good deal to spend in local stores. At that rate, it might take the average family several years to spend enough to earn a bicycle. Well, maybe that was just what the stamp plan was for, to encourage people to keep coming back to the same store over a long period of time.

The bicycle, costing thirty books at three dollars a book, was worth ninety dollars. That was rather high, but Ted decided it might be worth it. It certainly had everything, and it was hard to judge about bike prices. There were so many different models, and the price of foreign models was considerably influenced by the duty on them.

Let's see. If each book came to three dollars, and represented a hundred dollars in purchases, with a Blue Harvest stamp given for each dime, that meant a book ought to contain a thousand stamps. Just for the fun of it, with time hanging heavy on his hands, Ted decided to count up and see. And count he did. It couldn't be easily calculated, because some of the pages were partly filled with advertising and dummy stamps. These were printed "free" stamps, which the customer didn't have to cover.

Ted began to count, writing his figures down on a paper after every few pages so he wouldn't lose count. He wondered just how accurately he would come out. When he finished, his total should add up to a thousand stamps.

The spaces seemed endless. The books were going to take longer to fill than most people realized, unless they bought some big utilities. At last Ted had his column of figures, and ran down it. First column zero, second column zero—that was all right so far. But the third column—fifteen? No, that couldn't be right, it was only supposed to be ten. Ted frowned. He added it up again. It still came out fifteen hundred stamps.

Something was wrong here. He started over again. He went through the book carefully once more. This time there could be no doubt. A customer had to paste in fifteen hundred stamps in order to complete his book. Fifteen hundred stamps, at ten cents each, meant that the customer would have to spend a hundred and fifty dollars to fill a book.

But if he spent a hundred and fifty dollars to fill a book worth three dollars, then he was getting only 2 percent on his money. And Ted remembered very clearly that Mr. Woodring had told Mr. Dobson the plan paid 3 percent.

CHAPTER 5

EXPLANATIONS—OF A SORT

Offhand, the difference between 3 percent and 2 percent didn't sound like very much. But putting a cash value on it, if the plan paid 3 percent, he figured each book was worth four-fifty. If it paid 2 percent, each book was worth only three dollars. That meant that the customer was getting cheated out of a dollar and a half for every book he filled. Multiply this by the hundreds or thousands of books that were going to be filled, and this could turn out to be a good-sized racket.

Ted sat back, worried. He hated to see Mr. Dobson get mixed up in anything that wasn't just right. And it wasn't only Mr. Dobson, it was the whole town. Once let people get the idea there was something fishy connected with these stamps, and business would flow out of Forestdale and over to North Ridge in a steady stream.

But, then, where did all this leave Ted? He ought at least to talk it over with Mr. Dobson, he thought, though he didn't like the idea. It seemed as if he were going behind Mr. Woodring's back, the man with whom he was now associated. Of course if there was really anything wrong going on, he would have to tell—but wouldn't it be fairer all around to let Mr. Woodring make an explanation first? Maybe it was just a simple slip of the tongue, after all. Suppose the stamps did pay only 2 percent—maybe that was all any of the plans paid.

Mr. Woodring came in about four-thirty. He seemed to be in a hurry, as though he wanted to be sure Ted wouldn't have to work overtime. That was a very good point in his favor and made Ted feel more uncomfortable than ever about that difference in percent he had discovered. He wondered how he ought to lead up to it, but had no opportunity for a few minutes, because Mr. Woodring was looking very pleased about something.

"No more calls, Ted?"

"No—just the one I told you about."

"That's all right, Ted. We did a good day's work. That was the important call. It was from Mr. Kirtland."

Kirtland's—the largest store in Forestdale! If Mr. Woodring had them signed up, he had really made an important deal.

"But if that was Mr. Kirtland," Ted inquired, "why didn't he give me his name?"

"It wasn't necessary. That was his private number, so it didn't have to go through the switchboard. It made me feel kind of good, as though he really considered our plan important. So I made an appointment for this afternoon, we had a little discussion, and he signed right up. It was about the easiest customer I ever did sign. Some of the small shops often keep you dangling for months, and then the chances are they'll turn you down, after all."

Maybe it sounded easy, but Ted knew Mr. Kirtland by reputation to be a very careful, shrewd person. He must have looked into this plan pretty thoroughly before he put his signature on the contract. But could even a man like Mr. Kirtland have been fooled by that difference in percent? Mr. Woodring seemed to be so happy with the deal—in contrast to his bitter mood on the telephone earlier that day—that Ted hesitated to bring up his question.

"When does the plan start?" he asked.

"Tuesday morning. Mr. Kirtland's one of those persons who don't dillydally. Once he's made up his mind, that's it. There'll be an advertisement in Tuesday's *Town Crier,* and they'll begin giving out stamps the same day."

"Do you have enough stamps to get him started?" asked Ted, for there certainly weren't any around the office.

"Oh, yes. When I came out to Forestdale, I brought a big box of stamps with me. They're still unopened in my hotel room. I didn't want to leave them lying around, since they're worth several hundred dollars." He laughed. "Anyway, stamps tend to get all sticky when you don't handle them just right. Well, Ted, I don't think there's anything more you have to do around here. You can go now, if you like."

"Then I'll see you tomorrow morning." Ted's tone was half-questioning.

"Saturday morning? Oh, I don't think it'll be necessary for you to come in tomorrow, Ted. I don't have any appointments, so I'll be puttering around in here myself all morning, and I can handle anything that comes up. I'm not looking for much on a Saturday. See you Monday, then."

Still Ted hesitated, not quite liking to leave things hanging as they were. He had hoped Mr. Woodring would give him an opening so that he could ask questions, but he hadn't. He would have to plunge in himself, and he took a deep breath.

"Mr. Woodring, just how much is one of these books of stamps worth, anyway?"

Mr. Woodring had been straightening up some papers on the desk, but at Ted's question he spun about, a frown on his face.

"You mean its redemption value?"

"Yes."

"Why, I thought I explained to you, Ted, that the plan pays 3 percent, as far as the customer is concerned."

"Yes, that's what I thought you said, Mr. Woodring. But I counted up the stamps in a book, and now it looks to me as if this whole thing pays only 2 percent."

"You counted them?" Mr. Woodring's voice was very deliberate and restrained. "And what did you figure out from that?"

"Well, according to the premiums, each book is worth three dollars. Take this doll, for instance"—Ted nodded toward the window display—"you can get it by redeeming five books, so that makes it worth fifteen dollars. At 3 percent there ought to be a thousand stamps in a book, but there are actually fifteen hundred."

"You're mistaken, Ted," said Mr. Woodring calmly. "Each completed book is really worth four-fifty in merchandise. That doll is a twenty-two-fifty doll."

Ted's eyes narrowed. Mr. Woodring sounded very glib and sure, but Ted had made up his mind not to be taken in by anything, and he had figured out the plan paid only 2 percent. Of course it was hard to tell about the doll. It might be a fifteen-dollar doll, or it might be a twenty-two-fifty doll, for all Ted knew. But the bicycle was different.

"Then how much is that bicycle worth?" asked Ted carefully.

"What does the premium catalogue say?" replied Mr. Woodring with a careless air. "Five books plus seventy-five dollars? Each book is worth four-fifty, so five books would be worth twenty-two fifty.

Add that on to the seventy-five, and you get ninety-seven fifty. That's the value of the bicycle."

Having already decided that the bicycle was worth ninety dollars, Ted found himself stubbornly unwilling to change his ideas. Anyway, there was another way to figure it.

"What about a person who pays for the bicycle entirely in stamps? Thirty books, at four-fifty a book, would make the bicycle worth a hundred and thirty-five dollars. That couldn't be right, could it?"

"Hardly," said Mr. Woodring dryly. "I have already told you the bike was worth ninety-seven fifty. You're a very discerning young man, Ted, and I can see now why Mr. Dobson hired you for my assistant. I'm glad to have you asking all these questions, because as my assistant you have to have all this information at your fingertips. However, the average person saving stamps isn't going to go into all these details.

"Now I'll tell you how the difference in the two values of the bicycle comes about. We *say* that the bicycle can be obtained for thirty books, but out of our experience we *know* that no family is going to save that long. It would just take too darn long, and children, especially, get impatient when they have to wait for things. The average family saving for a bicycle will complete five books, then come in and pay the seventy-five dollars to go with them. That's exactly what we expect them to do, and what we *want* them to do. If we can get people to buy our merchandise with both stamps *and* cash, we're going to have a much larger turnover than if we have to depend on stamps alone.

"Although the bicycle should be obtainable for no more than twenty-two books, my company has made it thirty books. One reason for this is that we want to encourage people to pay part in cash. The other reason is that in some states there are taxes on plans like this, and in order to make a tax saving it's to our advantage to put as low a value on these stamps as possible. That's why we say, when filing a tax report, that each book is worth three dollars. Maybe that sounds like cheating, but merchandise values are not fixed, and there's no reason why my company should cheat itself."

Ted's attention had turned back to the doll. "If a person were going to buy a doll like that, would he really have to pay twenty-two fifty for it?"

"That's a wonderful doll, Ted. A lot more handwork goes into a product like that than most people realize. I'll tell you something about our premiums, Ted. We're not anxious to compete against the local stores. We handle only quality items. You couldn't buy that doll in Kirtland's because they don't handle it. You see, it's more than most people would want to pay for a doll. The same is true of the bicycle. And that coffee maker—you'll notice that it's a larger size than most families use.

"Kirtland's don't handle that doll, because it's too expensive, and there wouldn't be enough demand for it. That means that Kirtland's couldn't buy it in quantity lots. If you *did* order that doll through Kirtland's, you'd have to pay at least twenty-two fifty for it. That doesn't mean *my* company must sell it for twenty-two fifty. Our stamp plan works all over the country. That means we *can* buy this doll in quantity, and at a discount, and we can afford to sell it at less than twenty-two fifty. Just the same, it's only fair to say the real price is twenty-two fifty, when that is what people would have to pay locally."

His explanation was rather long and involved, but he had been patient about it. Now he snapped his jaw shut, as though he would rather not be asked any more questions about the matter. As for Ted, although he had understood most of what Mr. Woodring said, he felt his head swirling with figures. He didn't want to go to Mr. Dobson right now—not until he'd had a chance to think over all these things. At the same time, he wanted to let Mr. Woodring know that he *might* talk it over with the editor.

"If I should see Mr. Dobson, Mr. Woodring, is it all right for me to tell him about this? He might be confused about that 3 percent, as I was."

"Certainly, Ted. You're working for him—that was our agreement. I hope you understand it all, though. Don't do anything to get matters more confused. If Mr. Dobson wants to talk to me about it, I'll be glad to discuss it with him."

"O.K.," Ted agreed, laughing. "It is a pretty mixed-up thing, isn't it?"

"Sure is, Ted. Good night. See you Monday," but Mr. Woodring's voice, though apparently cheerful, seemed just a little restrained, and Ted figured that he might have been a little resentful of Ted's questions. Well, by Monday morning it would probably have all blown over. Meanwhile, Ted was beginning to like his new job. If nothing else, he was beginning to learn a good deal more about retail trade.

Ted's date with Nancy on Saturday failed to come off, after all. She telephoned that night apologetically. Her aunt had planned a weekend trip out of town.

"I'm awfully sorry, Ted. But Aunt Marian bought the tickets as a kind of surprise for me, before she found out about our date. Of course we could turn them in, but—"

"Oh, that's perfectly all right, Nancy. I know you'll have a good time, and we can postpone our date."

"Thanks for the rain check, Ted." She paused, as though waiting for him to set another date.

Ted was about to mention the following Saturday, but remembered the gang was planning something for that night, and he'd better wait to make sure he could get Nancy included. "I'll call you next week, Nancy."

"All right, Ted. Good-by." But she still sounded a little disappointed, for which Ted was not sorry. Better disappointed than indifferent.

With an emptier weekend than he had anticipated, Ted found his thoughts returning to that difference in the percentages he had discovered. Mr. Woodring's explanations *had* been rather smooth and convincing, but away from the office Ted wasn't so sure any more. When he had figured the plan out at 2 percent and the books worth three dollars each, everything had come out so evenly. When he tried to figure things differently, at 3 percent and the books worth four-fifty, it took a lot of explanations to make up the difference.

Maybe the explanations *were* real, but Ted, being inexperienced in the field, found himself unable to decide for sure. Anyway, the conviction began to grow upon him that he ought at least to report the matter to Mr. Dobson. The editor would understand things more clearly, and was in a better position to decide if there was anything crooked about this stamp plan—and to do something about it if there were. Yes, it was an unpleasant duty, but Ted couldn't see how to get out of it.

But not on Saturday morning. There was too much of a rush around the *Town Crier* as they tried to close the office by noon (they seldom made it). Anyway, it was past noon before Ted had fully made up his mind. But he wouldn't put it off any longer than Monday. First thing he would stop down at the *Town Crier* office. Mr. Dobson was usually at his desk before the rest of the staff or even the printer had come in. Ted could talk things over with him in private—and incidentally could avoid another meeting with Carl Allison. Then, with this decision made, Ted tried to put the matter out of his mind.

Another telephone call came for him early Saturday evening. It was from Margaret Lake.

"Ted, did you hear what it was we'd planned?"

"Well, I heard you were planning *something,* " Ted admitted.

"It's going to be a hayride, Ted—next Saturday night. We wanted something unusual, and we thought it might be kind of exciting."

"Sure will be," Ted agreed. "I'll be looking forward to it."

This was true, but at the same time it was beginning to get a little embarrassing, for Ted and Margaret had gone to the prom together.

"Ted, how would you like to bring Nancy Lindell?"

"Well," said Ted, a little uncomfortably, "why don't you and I go together, and Nelson could take Nancy?"

"Because she's a stranger in town, and you're the only one who knows her well enough to invite her. Anyway, what difference does it make who goes with whom? We'll all be together on the wagon, and it'll be a community lunch. I can ask Nelson—"

"I don't think he'd go with you," said Ted doubtfully.

"How come?"

"Well, he'd think he might be pushing me out of the picture."

"Oh, nuts! Why does every simple thing have to turn out to be so complicated? All right, I'll ask Cliff Corby, and Jane can ask Nelson. You don't play a musical instrument, do you?"

"I used to play the rhythm sticks in the kindergarten."

"That's a big help! Maybe we can get someone with a guitar or an accordion. I don't think a portable radio would be half so good. Nine o'clock Saturday, then, at the Smithdale farm, and all parents warned we don't know when we'll be back."

Her voice sounded very gay as she hung up, and Ted was relieved. Of course he had known that Margaret would be understanding about Nancy—simply because she was that sort of girl.

CHAPTER 6

AN INCIDENT ON THE ROAD

Early Monday morning found Ted in the Town Crier office, explaining as carefully as he could about his discovery. Mr. Dobson listened very carefully, a worried frown on his face.

"I don't know, Ted," said the editor, when Ted had concluded. "It's something very hard to judge. When you are handling merchandise that is non-competitive, you can put almost any price on it you please. Your only limitation is the price people are willing to pay, and one of the things about this stamp plan is that people don't know exactly what they *are* paying."

"But isn't there some way of finding out for certain whether the stamps pay 2 percent or 3 percent?" asked Ted anxiously. Time was running out, he knew. The Kirtland advertisement would be on its way to the presses in a few hours, and after that the newspaper would be committed to the Blue Harvest stamp plan, whether they liked it or not.

"Oh, yes, there's a very simple way." Mr. Dobson smiled. "All I have to do is call up Mr. Kirtland and ask him what price his store is paying for the stamps."

Ted grinned, too, amazed that he hadn't thought of such a simple plan. This should settle it once and for all. He watched as Mr. Dobson dialed a number, and because the call went through directly to Mr. Kirtland, Ted knew that Mr. Dobson also had Mr. Kirtland's private number.

"He's an early riser, too," the editor explained with his hand over the mouthpiece as he waited for the phone to ring. "Oh, hello, Mr. Kirtland? This is Chris Dobson. I wanted to get clear on the price you're paying for the Blue Harvest stamps."

At last Mr. Dobson put down the receiver, and turned to Ted, frowning.

"Things aren't too good, Ted. Mr. Kirtland is paying only 2 percent for the stamps. It simply isn't reasonable that the stores would pay only 2 percent for the stamps and that the Blue Harvest company would then redeem them at 3 percent. I'm very much afraid that three dollars is more nearly the correct value of a book of stamps, and that Mr. Woodring has been selling you a bill of goods."

Ted's face fell. When once he had found out a person was lying to him, he was inclined to lose confidence altogether.

"What do we do now?" asked Ted, discouraged. He was hoping Mr. Dobson would tell him he didn't have to go back to Mr. Woodring's office again.

"Let's think this through very carefully, Ted," the editor cautioned. "I admit that if I'd had this information a week ago I would have been much more careful about endorsing the plan. But now that I have endorsed it, it's pretty hard for me to back out, unless I can produce definite evidence of fraud."

"He said the plan paid 3 percent, and it pays only two," said Ted bitterly.

"All right, he said that to *us,* but he didn't say that to Mr. Kirtland or to the other stores, as far as I know. He isn't telling the store customers the plan pays 3 percent. It isn't on any of the newspaper advertising, or the store displays. So, then, who's getting cheated? Mr. Kirtland is perfectly satisfied. He's much more familiar with merchandising than I am, and he believes that his customers will be getting good value for their stamps."

"Mr. Woodring explained it to me as 3 percent," Ted pointed out, "and I was supposed to say the same thing to people who inquired."

"No, Ted, I don't think so. I think Mr. Woodring, in a first burst of enthusiasm, told us the plan was 3 percent. He must have been desperately anxious to get the newspaper's support in order to start the plan in Forestdale. You've noticed that he's not a very smooth person. He's not only new at the job—for of course Blue Harvest is a rather new firm—but the whole business is new to him. Of course he never dreamed that you'd sit down and try to figure out the percentage yourself. And notice that he never repeated to anyone that the plan paid 3 percent, until you put him on the spot, and he felt he had to make some sort of explanation. I think as far as Mr. Woodring is concerned he'd like to forget that whole 3 percent business. Let's just chalk it up to excess enthusiasm."

"But the stamps really do pay only 2 percent."

"Yes, Ted, I don't think there can be much question about that. Mr. Woodring's explanation reminds me of a person trading in a used car on a new car. The dealer may give an extra allowance on the old car but add the same amount on to the price of the new car. Mr. Woodring wants to raise the value of the stamps, while he also raises the price of his premiums."

"And five books still buy a doll, no matter what the books and the doll are worth."

"Exactly, Ted."

"Then what do we do, go on just as though nothing has happened?"

"I wish we could, Ted." The editor considered. "As long as he doesn't repeat this 3 percent business to anyone else, I think we can drop that angle. No, there's something else that worries me much more. Here's a letter I got in this morning's mail."

As he took it from the envelope, Ted saw that it had come by air mail. Somebody must have been in a hurry about something.

Mr. Dobson took out the letter and reread it before explaining to Ted. "It's from that friend of mine, at Beacon, Jones and Western in Chicago. He tells me that Mr. Woodring was not employed ten years ago by either Beacon and Jones or by Western."

"Then he really is lying, after all," said Ted, with a kind of tired conviction.

"Yes, I'm afraid it is a lie, Ted, but just how important a lie it is I don't know. After all, Mr. Woodring didn't give us any written statement that he was employed there, and whether he was or not has very little bearing on his stamp plan. Perhaps he merely made an idle remark."

"But when you deliberately say something that's not true at all—"

"Well, Ted, I don't say I like it. But, as I said, Mr. Woodring is new at the business, and he may have thought he could earn my confidence by making some such casual remark without dreaming I had a way of checking up on him. No, I don't discount a man altogether, just because he told some small lie that doesn't seem to have any importance anyway. I wish it hadn't happened, but it still doesn't change the stamp situation. The people behind the plan are reliable, and Mr. Kirtland is satisfied."

"Then you're going on with the campaign?"

"Yes, Ted, I don't think there's anything else I can do. At the same time I appreciate very much that you brought this matter to my attention, and I'm glad I've got you there, just in case anything else of this kind comes up. However, just one thing more would be the last straw, as far as I'm concerned. You can forgive a few small mistakes, but you don't have to go on until they add up to one big mistake."

Since it was time for Ted to be getting to work, he said good-by and left, just as Miss Monroe and Nancy arrived. He wanted to ask Nancy about the hayride, but he was late, and he didn't like to ask her in front of the others, anyway.

"I'll call you tonight, Nancy," he promised.

"All right, Ted, I'll be waiting."

At the office Mr. Woodring seemed as cordial as ever, having either overlooked or forgotten the tension between them on the previous Friday. He was in a hurry, however, and after giving Ted a few instructions for the day, took his leave. He returned a moment later, to give Ted a key to the office, as he had promised.

"Sorry, Ted, but this is my only key. You'll be able to get out for lunch, but I guess you'll have to wait till I get back before going home."

This was all right with Ted, since this is what he would have preferred to do anyway. The morning proved fairly busy. A number of telephone inquiries came in. He was able to steer several persons toward making an appointment, some simply wanted information that Ted was able to supply at once, and two had more complicated questions. Ted promised them that he would look up the information himself, or if he was unable to get it, ask Mr. Woodring and call back with it as soon as he could. Tracking down this information through the various leaflets Mr. Woodring had left took him quite a while, and he was not yet finished when Nelson stopped in, just a few minutes before noon.

"Thought we'd have lunch together," Nelson remarked, "or are you too busy to eat?"

"Oh, I'm never that busy," Ted admitted, glancing at the clock. "I wanted to get this done before noon, but I guess I can't, so we might as well go now, if you want to."

Ted locked up, and after a little discussion about where they ought to eat, they got Into Nelson's car, and he drove toward a roadside stand a few miles out of town which was a favorite spot for their crowd.

"Did you get your invitation to the hayride all right?" Nelson inquired.

"Yes. I'm taking Nancy, if she'll go with me. Who are you going with?"

"Jane Yuleson. I don't know how she came to ask me. I've never been out with her before."

"Oh, I guess the girls must have parceled us out among themselves," said Ted with a grin, but not explaining his conversation with Margaret.

"That's pretty good, a hayride. I thought all the farms around here were mechanized. I wonder why Mr. Smith keeps horses?"

"Probably to rent them out to hayride parties. Say, are you sure his name is Smith? I thought it was Smithdale."

"That's the name of his farm. His name is Smith."

Nelson drove on in silence for a moment. "Listen, Ted, if it's none of my business, just say so, but how are you and Margaret running along? Is Nancy breaking you up?"

"Oh, no, nothing like that. Margaret knows she comes first with me. But with college and everything facing us, we're not ready to get tied down yet."

Arriving at the spot, Nelson guided the car into a narrow parking space to the side of the restaurant. They found a few of their friends inside and during the conversation that followed—a general, confused conversation that quickly jumped from one topic to another— mention was made of the Blue Harvest stamps. Ted was asked how soon the plan was going into effect.

"Tomorrow morning," he informed them. "Read all about it in the *Town Crier*—."

Then an argument developed over the merits of such stamp plans, with the girls inclined to be in favor and the boys opposed. Ted was asked for his opinion.

"I'm neutral," he replied good-naturedly. "If it works, I'm for it. We'll have to wait and see."

Then the conversation took a different turn, and the stamps were forgotten.

After returning to the office, Ted was able to complete the jobs he had begun before lunch and called back the parties with good results. They, too, were now ready to make appointments, and Ted felt he would have good news for Mr. Woodring. He arrived about four o'clock, which was a little earlier than Ted had expected him, and was pleased with Ted's report.

"Looks like things are beginning to take hold. Ted, I'm not through for the day yet. I'm on my way over to North Ridge, and I thought you might like to ride along."

"Sure thing," Ted agreed quickly, "only I thought you didn't expect to get much business in North Ridge."

"Not from the big stores, but some of the little places are feeling the effects of the stiff competition they're getting and are looking rather desperately for some gimmick to help them stay in business. I'm all for efficiency, but when I can see a way to help the little fellow, I think that's a pretty worth-while thing, too. I have an appointment with the editor of the *News-Record,* to see what sort of help he'll be willing to give me. You're acquainted with people on the paper there, aren't you?"

"Well, I only know the editor by sight. But I'm a friend of Ken Kutler's, and he's their reporter."

"Yes, I thought it was something like that. That's why I suggested you might like to come along."

They found Ken Kutler just emerging from the office, and Ted introduced the men. Having heard further details of then-long friendship, Mr. Woodring suggested that Ted stay and talk to Ken while he went inside. Ted found himself liking the man in spite of those nagging little doubts in the back of his mind.

"Well, Ted, how goes it?" asked Ken when they were alone.

"Oh, not very much stirring. Anything doing with you?"

"Not a thing. This is the dullest summer I've ever gone through. You're not holding out on me, are you, Ted? There's nothing big you're trying to cover up?"

"No danger." Ted grinned. "If there were, you'd have had wind of it by this time."

"Well, I'll repeat what I've said before, Ted. If we do come up against each other, it'll be no holds barred this time. But it doesn't look as though anything will come up in the few weeks you'll still be in town."

"Then you'll still have Carl Allison to worry about," Ted reminded him.

"Allison?" Ken rubbed his chin thoughtfully. "I haven't yet felt I had to worry about him, though you never can tell. The way I look at Allison right now, he's just a person who's holding a newspaper job. I don't know yet whether he's a real newspaperman."

"How will you be able to tell?" asked Ted.

"Oh, there'll be signs—plenty of them. It's kind of hard to explain, Ted. But I guess the best word I can find to describe it is *class*. If he's got class, the kind of class that shows a person really belongs, it'll show up sooner or later. And if he hasn't got it, that'll soon show up, too. When I find out for sure, I'll let you know."

They talked over family affairs and past experiences for a while, until Mr. Woodring came out of the office. Then the men shook hands again, and Ted and Mr. Woodring drove off.

"It didn't take long," Ted observed. "Good news?"

"Good enough, Ted. He's going to give us some publicity, and that's all I could reasonably expect. The way I feel about it, this has been a highly satisfactory day. You didn't find much time to read today, did you?"

Ted shook his head. "No, I didn't, although I hadn't planned to, anyway. I thought it mightn't look right."

"I wouldn't have minded, but just the same I'm glad you were so busy you didn't have time. I keep a couple of books in my glove compartment, just in case I find myself with a little time to kill."

"Do you do quite a bit of reading, Mr. Woodring?"

"I used to, when I was younger and had more time for it."

Ted ventured a more personal question. "Have you had a vacation this summer, Mr. Woodring?"

"Well, I was between jobs for a while early in the summer, if you call that a vacation. I've got a little cabin back up in the hills"—he made a jerking motion with his head—"that's a wonderful place to relax. I think it's one of the most beautiful spots in the world—a little green plateau beneath a cliff overlooking two waterfalls. You can almost toss a bare hook into the mountain stream and get all the fish you can eat. There's hunting, too, although I've never cared much for that. Luckily the tourists haven't found it yet. When they do, it'll be spoiled."

"Then I won't ask you where it is," said Ted, grinning.

"Well, it's—"

Whatever Mr. Woodring intended to say was lost as he suddenly swerved the car and slammed on the brake. The car bounced crazily for a moment, but came to a safe stop several feet from the ditch which bordered the road. It all happened so quickly that Ted had no time to feel frightened.

"What was it?" he asked.

"Some small animal—I couldn't quite tell what it was—in the shadow of that little dip in the road."

"Whatever it was, it's gone now," Ted remarked, turning his head to stare out the window.

Carefully Mr. Woodring backed the car out onto the road, and they drove on at a somewhat slower rate.

"That was a reckless thing to do," he decided. "It's just that I've always liked animals—I always had some sort of pet when I was a kid. I have to apologize to you, Ted."

"No, you don't. I understand. I like animals, too."

The incident was not mentioned again, but Ted felt mixed up about Mr. Woodring. Certainly a man who would risk his own life to save some unknown animal crouching in the dip of a dusky road must have some fine qualities even though you couldn't believe everything he said.

CHAPTER 7

WHAT COLOR IS THE COW?

When ted called Nancy that evening, he found her enthusiastic about the hayride, but she brought up a point that bothered her.

"Ted, you're all friends—you've been to school together for years. And I won't know anybody there. Maybe they won't want a stranger."

"They wouldn't have told me to ask you if they didn't want you. Anyway, you'll be acquainted by then. I'll take you around a few places during the week, if you'll let me, and you'll get to know everybody."

"That would be fun, Ted. You said that the girls are planning the lunch? Maybe they'll let me help."

"I'll bet they'll be glad for all the help they can get."

This was the way things were arranged, and Ted found that Nancy fitted easily and pleasantly into their crowd. Though she came from a large and distant city and Forestdale was quite a small town, she didn't make comparisons. The others quickly accepted her, and she soon found herself treated as though she had been one of them for years.

On Tuesday morning Kirtland's announced the Blue Harvest plan with a full-page advertisement in the *Town Crier,* and there was also a news item about it on the front page. Mr. Dobson did not make a practice of tying in his news columns with the advertising, but in this case he evidently felt the Blue Harvest stamps were a legitimate item of news, something of concern to the whole town. Ted heard later from his mother that Kirtland's had done an unusual volume of business for a Tuesday.

Either through curiosity, or because she felt that loyalty to Ted and his new job required her to show interest in the plan, Mrs. Wilford was among the Kirtland customers that first day. The shirt she bought for Ted was something he didn't exactly need until it came time to leave for college, still a month off. When she showed Ted his new shirt, she also showed him the stamps she had received with the purchase. Ted immediately screwed up his eyes.

"Are those the stamps you got, Mom? They aren't blue. They're purple!"

"No, they're not, Ted. They're blue. Blue Harvest stamps. You can tell by the name."

Ted shook his head. "They still look purple to me."

"It's just the artificial fight in here, Ted. They'd look different by natural light."

At her urging Ted took the stamps out on the front porch. It was nearly twilight, so the light was not too good, but at the same time Ted didn't feel anything was changed. He still thought the stamps looked purple.

"Are you sure those stamps look blue to you, Mom?"

"Of course they do, Ted. It's not a pure, true blue, I admit, but it is blue. Maybe your eyes are tired from doing close work all day."

Ted admitted that he was a little tired, but he still didn't think that had anything to do with the color of the stamps. Well, he'd check with some of his friends when he saw them, and see what they thought.

He had a chance to ask Nelson the next day when he ran into him at noon.

"Got your stamps yet?" Ted called to him, as Nelson was driving past.

Nelson drew over to the curb and stopped. "Sure have."

"So you did break down. I thought you weren't going to have anything to do with these stamps."

"They're for my *mother,*" said Nelson with dignity.

"What about those stamps, Nel? What color do you think they are?"

"What color? Why, they're blue, of course. What'd you think? You blind or something?"

"Just checking. Let's have a look at them and see."

His friend drew the stamps from the bag he had with him and handed them over. To Ted they looked like the purple stamps his mother had showed him the night before.

"Where'd you get 'em?"

"Kirtland's, of course. That's the only outfit handling them so far, isn't it?"

"The only big one," Ted admitted.

Nelson got out of the car and looked at his friend as though he feared he had suddenly become demented.

"Something the matter with you, Ted? Don't these stamps look blue to you?"

"I'm afraid not," Ted disagreed. "They look purple to me."

Nelson looked more than ever puzzled. He held up the set of stamps and pointed. "This cow, here, does that look purple to you?"

"Sure, that's the most purple of all."

"Well, what do you know, a purple cow. Are you sure you weren't thinking about that poem about the purple cow, Ted, and that's why these stamps look purple to you?"

"No, I wasn't. Are you sure It isn't because you knew they were called Blue Harvest stamps that they look blue to you?"

"I don't think so. Who wrote that silly little poem about a purple cow, anyway?"

"Gelett Burgess, but I wasn't thinking of the poem."

"Well, I don't know, Ted." Nelson considered. "I've talked to a lot of people about these stamps, and nobody mentioned to me that they looked purple. What did your mother say about them?"

"Oh, she thought they looked blue, just as you do."

"Well, then, you can rely on that, Ted, because most women have more color sense than men do. You just find me a *girl* who thinks those stamps look purple, and I might begin to think you have something."

He studied Ted once more, as though his friend had suddenly become an interesting medical case. "You say these stamps look purple, Ted. Well, what kind of purple is it? Is it a brilliant, flaming purple?"

"Oh, no, nothing like that. Just an ordinary purple, with a kind of bluish cast. What sort of blue does it look like to you?"

"Well—just an ordinary kind of blue, with a little bit of a purplish cast."

They both laughed. "Well, maybe we're not so far apart, after all," Ted remarked.

"No," Nelson agreed. "A funny thing about color, though. How can I know what you're actually seeing, and how can you tell what

I'm actually seeing? Maybe we're both seeing the same thing, but we've each got a different name for it."

"Wait a minute." Ted thought of something. "I know how I can show you what I mean. Come on over to the office a minute."

At his urging, Nelson followed him across the street to the locked office. They stood outside for a moment, looking at the large poster illustrating the Blue Harvest stamp.

"There," Ted pointed out. "What color does that stamp look to you?"

"Why, it's blue, Ted—a deep, rich blue."

"Sure it is," said Ted with a growing excitement mounting within him. "Now would you say that's the same color blue that appears on the stamps?"

"Well, no," Nelson admitted with some reluctance. Then he suddenly laughed. "Oh, now I see what's the trouble. You've been looking at those posters so long you think that's the way those stamps ought to look, and you're disappointed. I don't think you could expect anything like that, Ted. You know how posters are always gaudier than the real thing. You couldn't expect to have those same brilliant colors by the time you've reduced the picture down to stamp size. You won't see any stamps like that."

"No, I guess not," Ted agreed slowly. "Well, I guess my cow wasn't purple after all."

"No," Nelson rejoined, "but come to think of it, a blue cow is just as queer as a purple cow, isn't it?"

* * * *

It was a busy and pleasant week for Ted. He buried his doubts, and things went well at the office. He and Nancy had fun during the evenings as he helped her get acquainted with his crowd.

On Saturday evening Nelson called for him. Then the boys picked up Nancy and Jane, and headed out toward the country. Twilight had just settled across the rolling farmland, and a big orange moon was lifting its head upon the eastern horizon.

"Full moon," Nelson gloated. "Did you girls plan that, too?"

"Well, we looked at the calendar just to make sure," Jane admitted.

It was a warm, still summer evening, without the trace of a cloud in the sky, and with some big hampers of food in the trunk, everything seemed in readiness for a perfect evening.

They found a circle of cars already in the farmyard. Cliff Corby drove up at about the same time as they did, and when he saw the other boys he almost exploded.

"Hey, what goes here?" He stepped out and they saw that he was wearing overalls, although all the rest were wearing sports coats and slacks. "I thought you girls said we were all going to wear overalls?"

"Why, no, Cliff, we said we *thought* about it," Helen Howland corrected him. "What's the difference? Maybe overalls *would* have been better."

"Sure," Nelson remarked, "and maybe if you're a good boy Farmer Smith will let you help drive the horses."

At that moment Mr. Smith led a horse out of the barn.

"Oh, a real racer!" one of the boys exclaimed. "You sure he won't run away?"

No answer, of course, was expected. It was a stolid old plow-horse, built for strength rather than speed, who looked as though he couldn't have run a step if he tried.

The team of horses was soon hitched up, and everybody climbed up into the hay. Mrs. Smith was coming along, too, and she got into the front seat beside her husband. There was some surprise when they actually began to move, as though they had doubted that a team of horses could pull a wagon as heavy as this.

"What do we do if these hayburners run out of gas?" someone asked.

"That's the trouble, they *can't* run out of gas. That's why they had to invent automobiles."

"Did anybody bring dill pickles?" called one of the girls. "It wouldn't be a picnic without dill pickles."

Fortunately there were plenty of dill pickles, as well as every other item of food customary on a picnic, including plenty of pop in a cooler.

"I didn't know hay itched like this," remarked Jane.

"Anybody that's got hay fever is in for a rough time."

The girls had done as well as they could in the musical department, coming up with an accordion, a harmonica, and a saxophone.

They sang and it soon became apparent to the others that Nancy had the best voice in the crowd, and she was urged to lead the singing. When things had quieted down afterward, it was suggested to Nancy that she ought to plan on a singing career.

"Oh, no, I know my voice isn't good enough for that. I do want to study music, though, and perhaps help other people to like music the way I do."

"Do you play a musical instrument?" she was asked.

"No, not really. We did have a kindergarten orchestra once, and I used to beat the sticks."

At this there was a wild howl of laughter, since it was well known that this was also Ted's only musical accomplishment.

"You two were made for each other," Nelson remarked. "Tell her about your purple cow, Ted, and see what she thinks."

Ted would just as soon not have had Nelson bring up the matter, but he carried through with it in good grace.

"Well, it just seemed to me that the cow on the Blue Harvest stamps looked more purple than blue."

"I thought so, too," said Nancy quickly. "It really is a purple cow."

"Wow! Now I've heard everything," Nelson exclaimed. "Are you sure you aren't saying that, Nancy, just to be polite?"

"Why, no. I mean," she explained quickly, "I think people should be polite. But if I agree with one person and disagree with a second person, I don't see how that's being more polite than if I disagreed with the first person and agreed with the second."

"Well, that's Nancy's opinion," said Nelson to the crowd in general. "Anybody else here think the cow's purple?"

There came a chorus of "No's," which seemed to make it pretty clear Ted and Nancy were in a minority. Then a voice came from the front seat which quieted down the crowd.

"You youngsters think there isn't any such thing as a purple cow? Well, let me tell you something. I've got a purple cow back on my farm."

"Now, David—"

His wife laid a restraining hand on his arm.

"Don't try to stop me, Amy. These kids nowadays are too skeptical about everything. It wouldn't hurt to let them know there are such things. Anybody wants to see my purple cow, just let 'em come out to see me. You, Ted—I think you'd be interested."

"Maybe I would," Ted agreed, but the whole crowd had become more subdued. They didn't quite know how to take the strange remark Mr. Smith had made. Of course they didn't really believe he had a purple cow—unless somebody had painted it purple. But since he claimed to have it, what could they say to contradict him?

"I didn't even know farmers had cows any more," said Jim with a laugh. "I thought maybe scientists had invented something new."

"No, I don't think they ever have invented anything as good as a cow, or that they ever will," Mr. Smith went on, paying no attention to his wife, who was trying to motion to him that he was talking too much for a young people's picnic. "That's what we need, a return to a more natural way of life. Now if—"

If he had intended a rather untimely lecture, he was interrupted as one of the horses seemed to falter, and he brought them to a sharp halt.

"What's the matter?" came several voices.

"Loose shoe, probably. I'll get down and take a look."

He did so, and his expectation was confirmed.

"What do we do now?" asked Cliff.

"Anybody got a spare?" came an unidentified voice.

"I guess Joe's done for the night," the farmer decided, "and I don't like to see old Amos try to handle the load alone. I've got another horse back at the farm, and we're not very far from home, because we've been traveling in a circle. How'd you young people like to wait while I lead Joe home and get another horse?"

"Alone in the dark?" asked Helen with a little shudder.

"The Dutch Mill's a little way up that hill. Why don't you put up there? You can take your lunch along and have your spread while you're wailing. We won't be more than an hour."

This met with a chorus of approvals. The passengers jumped down from the wagon and began to brush the hay from their clothing. The hampers of food were unloaded, along with the soft drinks. Mrs. Smith was to stay with the young people. Taking one of the lanterns from the wagon, the crowd started up the hill.

CHAPTER 8

THE DUTCH MILL

The Dutch Mill might have been transplanted from the Netherlands itself. It had been constructed by a Dutch immigrant family, as a close replica of the windmills found in their homeland. Although not very profitable, it perhaps helped to make the family feel at home, and it also made a picturesque addition to the countryside. It had been abandoned now for about a year when the family, with the children grown, had been obliged to make other living arrangements. Vacant though it was, it was not rundown property—at least not yet. The Dutch family had left it in neat order, and vandals had not touched it. There had been some talk of having Forestdale or one of the other nearby communities take it over and preserve it as public property, but so far nothing had been done.

The refugees from the hayride knew they would not be unwelcome there, for the doors were unlocked, and picnicking parties often came out that way for a holiday. The mill had an air of mystery about it, as most abandoned places do. Though the crowd may have doubted that any old-world spooks were still loitering about the place, it is probable that none of them would have cared to enter the place alone at night. However, in a group, it was a welcome adventure.

As they trudged up the hill, the mill loomed starkly above them, silhouetted against the night sky. The moon, so full and brilliant before, now seemed smaller and duller as it climbed higher in the sky. Although there was a light wind, the huge blades were not turning, but seemed to be creaking and tugging at some sort of brake that held them in position.

"What do they use windmills for?" Nelson inquired.

"Why, to pump water and grind up grain, don't they? Anyway, in Holland they do." This was Ted's observation.

"Sure, I know that. But what do they do when the wind stops?"

"Maybe it never stops in Holland. Even over here it doesn't stop completely as often as you might think."

"I don't know how they do it in Holland," Cliff stated scientifically, "but farmers in this country still use windmills to pump up water from a well and fill a tank, which they can draw on when they need it. But not big windmills like this one, that a family could live in. I guess they don't need them now, with electricity so cheap."

"Well, who wants to go in first?" asked Jim as they stopped in front of the door.

None of the girls cared for the honor, and having paved the way for a demonstration of his own bravery, Jim held the lantern high and pushed open the partly resisting door. There was a little scream from some of the girls as a flutter of wings was heard, and a bird sailed by close to their heads.

"Only a bat," Jim announced, though privately Ted doubted it, being under the impression that bats—not really birds—were more silent fliers than that. Anyway, nothing else followed, and the girls were persuaded to follow the boys inside. They found things neat and in good order, except for a few leaves that had drifted in, and an inevitable layer of dust. The bird may have been a straggler which accidentally came down the chimney, for no other wild life seemed to have found its way in.

"Well, let's get a fire built," Jim ordered, apparently having taken command. "You, Ted, stop daydreaming and get a move on. You're in charge of the fire detail."

It may be argued that Ted could hardly have been daydreaming at night, but at least he came to with a start. His thoughts had been wandering, and if he had been required to explain them he would have had to admit they centered around a purple cow. Nelson had almost talked him out of his notion that the cow was purple, but now Nancy had come along and claimed the same thing. And she couldn't have gotten the idea from the posters. Probably she had never seen them, and at least she hadn't stared at them all day as Ted had for the past week. She had denied that she was just being polite, and Ted didn't believe she was. That cow really did look purple to her and to Ted, but apparently to no one else. Why was that?

"Why do we need a fire?" asked Ted, but moved slowly toward the fireplace. Certainly the evening was warm enough, and as far as Ted knew they hadn't brought anything along that required cooking.

"Because—it'll make things more cheerful," Jim decided, although he had apparently just thought of his reason. He was a person more inclined to act than to think, and had made his decision that they ought to have a fire before having any logical excuse.

Ted began to clear out the fireplace and in a few minutes had a fire blazing. Margaret was there to help out, handing him the kindling, and she and Ted exchanged amused and understanding glances. She wasn't in the least jealous of Ted's attention to Nancy, for she realized that Ted's obligation to Miss Monroe required him to show Nancy around and help her become acquainted in town. The warm friendship Ted and Margaret had enjoyed for years was too solid to be disturbed by such a small thing.

Meanwhile the lunch had been spread out on a cloth on the wooden table, and the picnickers began to load up their paper plates and find a place to sit, either on the floor or on one of the two wooden benches grouped in a half circle around the flickering fire. Their shadows danced upon the opposite wall.

"Anybody know any ghost stories?" asked Jim.

The girls protested, but it was a girl who volunteered to tell the first story.

"This story happened to a lady," Helen began.

"Is it true?" Nelson demanded.

"Of course it's true," Jim broke in. "All ghost stories are true—or they're supposed to be while you're telling them. Go on, Helen."

"Well, this is about a lady who married a certain man. The man had been married before, but his wife had died. Anyway, his second wife came to live with him in the same house, and they had most of the same furniture they had had before. Even the chinaware was the same.

"However, this woman had received some wedding gifts of her own, and among them was a beautiful and very expensive silver cream pitcher and sugar bowl. The woman was anxious to use her own things as much as she could, but her husband wanted to leave everything the way it was. Whenever she suggested changing anything, he would say, 'Why change it? It's always been that way.' The woman found this rather annoying.

"Anyway, she decided there was at least one thing she could change. She would start using her own silver cream pitcher and sugar bowl, instead of the ones that went with the regular dishes. She didn't bother asking her husband about it, and as a matter of fact she didn't think he would even notice.

"Well, this family set the breakfast table before going to bed, the way some families do so there will be less confusion in the morning. So one night the wife filled her own bowl with sugar and put it out on the table. Then they went to bed. But when she got up in the morning, she found the silver bowl was back in the cupboard and the china bowl was sitting in the middle of the table.

"Of course she thought that her husband had changed it. However, he didn't mention it, and she didn't say anything about it either before he went off to work.

"It was quite a few weeks before she could bring herself to use the silver sugar bowl again, but all that time she had been brooding about it. She didn't see why she shouldn't be able to use some of her own dishes, and she still didn't think her husband would notice, for usually he was too busy reading the latest stock quotations at the breakfast table. So she thought she'd try it again. But when she got up in the morning the old china sugar bowl was on the table again. This time it puzzled her, because she had been watching her husband more closely, and she couldn't see when he had had a chance to switch the sugar bowls.

"A few weeks later she decided to try it once more. She carefully filled the silver sugar bowl and put it out on the table after her husband had gone to bed. Then up in the bedroom she put a little doorstop in front of the door. If her husband should open the door during the night, this little doorstop would be moved out of position. In the morning the doorstop was still in place, but when she got downstairs there was the china sugar bowl on the table.

"Well, the only explanation she could find was that her husband must have changed it and then carefully replaced the doorstop. Not long after that her husband had to go out of town for a week. She thought that, at least while he was gone, she could use her own dishes, so the first night she put out the silver sugar bowl. But in the morning when she got up the china sugar bowl was there on the table.

"By this time she was beginning to get very worked up. She didn't believe in ghosts, and she was sure that somehow someone was breaking into the house, though why anyone should do so just for the sake of changing the sugar bowls she couldn't understand. The next night she locked all the doors and windows very carefully and put out the silver sugar bowl once more. In the morning, nothing seemed disturbed. Everything was still carefully locked up—but the sugar bowls had been changed again.

"She decided she must have walked in her sleep and changed the bowls herself. Just to prove it, she determined to stay up all night and watch. So at the usual time of going to bed she filled the bowl, put it out, and then went into another room where she could watch the table through the door. She somehow managed to keep awake all night, and kept her eyes on that sugar bowl as steadily as she could.

"At last morning came, and there was the silver sugar bowl still on the table. She decided that she'd been pretty silly about the whole thing. Here she'd been making a big mystery about it, when all the time she had been walking in her sleep and changing it herself. Then she boiled some water and made herself some tea, and reached out to get a spoonful of sugar. And when she did, *she found that the sugar bowl was empty!*"

This ending was so unexpected that everyone had to laugh. Suddenly the laughter died in mid-air at the sound of a slight scuffle from the next room. Everyone was immediately alert, and they stared at the doorway. The boys especially were all tensed for action, ready to spring at whatever was threatening.

Just as the tension became almost unbearable, a small animal crept around the corner of the doorway. It stopped as it came into full view, then crouched down and arched its back, and gave out a gentle meow. It was a jet-black cat.

Everyone laughed, and someone scooped up the cat and put it on Margaret's lap, where it settled down and began to wash its face.

"Talk about your ghost stories!" Nelson exclaimed.

"Poor starving thing," Jane sympathized.

"What do you mean poor?" asked Jim. "That's no starving cat. It looks pretty well fed to me. Either it's been feeding itself, or else it just wandered off from one of the farms around here."

The cat certainly didn't look at all hungry, and in fact refused a little portion of sandwich meat someone offered it. They all felt relieved, although a black cat was certainly in keeping with the spirit of that ghostly atmosphere. Ted alone felt a continuing tension. How had the cat managed to get in here? he wondered. He had supposed the place to be closed up tight. If not, surely the squirrels and other wild animals would have overrun the place by this time.

"Well, let's go on with the show," Cliff suggested. "Anybody else got a story?"

"I have," said Nancy, a little hesitantly. "And it's a true story, too—I think."

"Sure, they all are. Well, go ahead; try to scare us."

"Oh, I don't think it's the kind of story that would scare anybody, although it's pretty puzzling, at least to me. Let me ask you first, what's the largest thing that any of you has ever lost?"

"I lost a dollar once," Jim spoke up, "and it looked pretty big to me at the time."

"You mean something really big?" asked Nelson. "I lost my bicycle once—but I think it was stolen."

"And I forgot where I parked my car one time, and had to hunt for it for a while," Jim added.

"I lost my aunt's fur coat I borrowed for a dance," Jane recollected. "It was a lucky thing for me I found it, too, or I'd be paying for it yet."

"Is that all?" asked Nancy. "Hasn't anybody lost anything bigger than that?"

"I lost a trailer I was pulling once," Cliff put in, "but of course I didn't really lose it. I felt it give when it came off. Good thing I wasn't on a grade at the time."

"Let Nancy tell her story," Margaret suggested. "Let's see if she has lost something bigger than a trailer."

"Yes, I think I did," Nancy related. "The truth is, I think I've lost a whole town!"

"A whole town!" Ted exclaimed. "How could anybody lose a whole town?"

"That's just it. I really can't explain it. Look, has anybody heard of Freeport?"

"I know several Freeports," Jim maintained. "There's one in Illinois—"

"I know," said Nancy quickly, "but I want a Freeport in this state. Has anybody ever heard of it?"

They all shook their heads. "How do you know there is one?" asked Ted.

"Because my grandmother used to be mayor of it. I have some old letters to prove it. When I came to Forestdale for a visit, I hoped I'd be able to visit my grandmother's old town, but now I find that nobody's even heard of it."

Just then there was an unmistakable noise over their heads. Everyone grew quickly silent and alert.

"Quiet," Jim cautioned in a whisper. "There's somebody upstairs."

CHAPTER 9

A TOWN THAT DISAPPEARED

Except for the main room in which they found themselves, and a quick look into the adjoining room from which the cat had come, they had not bothered to explore the mill before settling down to their lunch and storytelling. Now they almost wished they had. Everything was silent once more upstairs, but there could be no doubt they had heard some sort of disturbance, and one that apparently could have been caused only by a human being.

The stairway, they found, was in the next room, and taking the lantern, the boys gathered in a group around the foot.

"Someone's up there, all right," Jim asserted. "Want to go up and rout him out?"

"Why don't we let well enough alone?" suggested Ted. "Whoever it is has probably got as much right here as we have."

"No, I don't agree with that, Ted, because we're here openly, and he's sneaking around about it."

"Then let's go!" suggested Cliff.

"He may have a gun," Ted cautioned them. He didn't care to appear chicken, and was in fact as eager for the adventure as any of the others, but he felt it better to point out all the possible consequences before plunging in.

"I think we can handle that part of it," said Nelson with confidence. "Anyway, we've got to find out, or afterward we'll all die of curiosity."

"Sure," added Jim, "and besides, we don't want him sneaking up on *us*."

"Keep the girls back, anyway," Cliff reminded them. As a matter of fact, none of the girls showed any great desire to be included. They had followed the boys as far as the doorway but had not come into the room.

"I don't think you boys ought to go up," said Mrs. Smith, but feeling that she had less authority over the boys than she did the girls, she added, "but if you're going, we'll wait by the fire. Come on, girls."

The girls followed her back to the fireside, leaving the boys to their own devices.

"I'm all for this," Nelson assured the others, "but at the same time let's not do anything silly. I want to know what's going on, but if it turns out he does have a gun, let's not try to rush him—unless we get a good chance."

"Let's stop talking and go!" said Jim impatiently.

He led the way, the others following close behind. They had tried to be quiet, but realized almost at once that no matter how quiet they tried to be, the person upstairs could hear them coming. Recognizing this, they became less careful, although they still strained their ears for any repetition of the sound they had heard before.

The long stairway took a turn halfway up, and just as Jim, who was in the lead, reached this landing they did hear another noise.

"Come on!" cried Jim, losing all caution. "He's opening a window."

He rushed ahead, the others at his heels. There was a series of rooms upstairs, so that they were confused for a moment, not being sure of the right one.

"Over there!" Jim decided, accurately enough the others agreed, and they rushed pell-mell toward the door and flung it open. The room was empty, but the window opposite was open, and they were just in time to catch a thud from the ground below.

"He must have dropped from the window sill!" exclaimed Nelson. "Let's go down."

The others rushed once more for the stairs, but Ted lingered behind. He felt they were too late to catch whoever it was now, and the more important thing was to try to catch some glimpse that would either help identify him or give some clue about what he was up to.

Leaning out the window, he did see someone—a man, he supposed—his figure indistinct in the shadows. He may have been stunned for just a moment from his fall, but he was on his feet in a second and streaking off for the nearby woods. Then, as Ted watched, the other boys arrived outside, waving the lantern about.

"He ran that way!" Ted called from the window, and with a shout of glee they took up the pursuit. Although he almost wished he was with them, Ted felt that the chase was useless. The man had had a sufficient head start to lose himself completely in the thick under-brush. The boys were soon lost to view, except that every once in a while the lantern flashed into sight momentarily. They seemed to be getting farther and farther afield, veering away from where Ted had seen the man disappear. He didn't think they had much prospect for success.

The room was now in darkness, except for the illumination from the moon. It was light enough by the window, but it took a while for Ted's eyes to adjust to the blackness before he could see anything else at all. The room was completely empty, which had been his first impression as they rushed in. He wasn't sure of its original purpose. It might have been simply a storeroom, particularly if the mill had ever been used for working purposes. But it seemed to Ted that the mill had been designed merely as a picturesque sort of residence, and that this was probably a bedroom.

Anyway, it was a south room. The full moon hung almost in front of the window and cast a faint yellow glow across the field. A weird effect at night, it must have been a beautiful view by day, Ted thought, with the barns and fields and distant hills. He decided to close the window, in order to keep out the birds and squirrels. The one bird and cat which they had found inside, he decided, must have gotten in while the intruder had the door open.

He couldn't stay any longer, and he groped his way downstairs, where he found the girls huddled about the fire in a somewhat fright-ened group. They had heard too much not to guess what was going on, and Ted told them as much as he knew.

"Are you sure there's no one still up there?" asked Jane tremu-lously.

"No," Ted replied, meaning he wasn't sure, but the girls took it for reassurance, and seemed to relax and to talk more freely and excitedly.

Then Ted stepped outside, waiting for the other boys to return from the chase. They hove into sight presently, out of breath but still pleased with the excitement of the hunt.

"No sign of him?" Ted questioned.

"No, not even a glimpse," Nelson responded. "You sure you really saw somebody, Ted?"

"Oh, I saw somebody, all right, but not well enough to identify him."

"It was a man, wasn't it? I mean, not just some kid."

"It looked like a man. Somebody pretty big, anyway."

"I wonder who it was?" Cliff speculated.

"Oh, just some tramp who decided to come in and spend the night," Jim decided. "Probably wanted to get out of the rain."

"What rain?" Nelson demanded. "It doesn't look like rain to me."

"Well, how did he know whether it might rain by morning? He probably didn't read the weather report."

"I guess it must have been a tramp, all right," Cliff agreed. "We're not far from the railroad tracks here, and the way he was headed he must have been trying to get back to the tracks, as though he knew his way around there. I wonder why tramps always hang around railroads, anyway?"

"That's about the only way they can get free transportation," Ted pointed out. "Who'd give a tramp a ride on a highway? And even if he walks, he might be arrested for vagrancy."

"Well, the way he lit out of here, I don't think he was up to much good. Why'd he take fright and run that way? He might have broken his leg, dropping from that window."

"How'd he know he wouldn't be arrested for trespassing? He couldn't be sure we weren't the owners."

"Well, just the same I wish we'd caught him. It would have been more fun—and the girls would have thought we were heroes."

"Maybe dead heroes," said Nelson gloomily.

They re-entered the mill, and for a few minutes there was some excited talk about the intruder. When things had quieted down a little, Nelson suggested:

"Why don't we look the place over? We haven't been in all the rooms."

There were some ayes and nays, but Mrs. Smith urged them not to.

"I don't think there's anyone else here, but even if there is, there's no sense looking for trouble. Anyway, I think my husband's back by now, and there's no use letting something like this spoil our fun."

With this the others reluctantly agreed. They began the task of gathering up the remains of their lunch and leaving the place as neat as they had found it. Upon leaving the mill, they could tell by the light of a lantern on the road that Mr. Smith had returned, and they speedily climbed up on the wagon once more. They attempted to restore their old gaiety, but they were more tired now, and their thoughts kept returning to the incident of the Dutch Mill.

"Just to think," said Jane with a shudder, "that we were enjoying our lunch all the time that man was in there."

"And even our medal-winning sprinter couldn't help us catch him," Cliff remarked. "I always suspected that stop watch was wrong."

"Maybe it was an hour slow," added Jim, grinning at the scowling Nelson.

There was more singing, more joking and chatter, but by the time another hour had passed they were all ready to head for home.

"Not much stamina, these young people," said Mr. Smith with a shake of his head, but nodding toward his wife. "We used to stay out till dawn."

Upon arriving back at the farm, they climbed out of the wagon, brushed themselves off, and began to gather their things together.

"Don't forget about my purple cow, Ted," the farmer called after him. "You'll have to come out and see her when you've got time."

"I'll remember," Ted promised, without exactly promising to come. His curiosity was beginning to mount, however. Why *did* Mr. Smith keep insisting that he had a purple cow, and what made him think that Ted in particular would be interested? It was just one more incident to file away in the back of his mind.

"We had a wonderful time, Mrs. Smith," he called. "Maybe we'll be doing this again sometime."

"We were glad to have you, Ted, and all the others. Come back soon."

With that the party broke up, and cars began to file out of the farmyard. Ted was with Nancy in the back seat of Nelson's car, as before.

"Well, I'd say we had a pretty good time, wouldn't you, Ted?" asked Nelson.

"Sure did."

"These girls planned a real shindig for us. We'll have to plan something back. How long before you leave town, Ted?"

"About another couple of weeks yet."

"Well, that'll give us some time. You'll be here for a while, too, won't you, Nancy?"

"Oh, yes, I'll stay as long as I can. I'm still looking for my lost town."

"I'll drop Nancy off first, Ted. Then I'll take you home, if you want me to."

"No, thanks," said Ted happily. "I can walk, and maybe Nancy will let me talk with her for a while."

They got out in front of her apartment house, and Nelson drove off amid an exchange of good nights. Ted and Nancy stood on the sidewalk for a moment, then walked slowly toward the steps. They were home earlier than expected, and there didn't seem any particular reason to hurry.

"Did you mean it, Nancy, about losing a town, or was that just a story?"

"No, I've really lost it, Ted. It's hard for me to understand what happened to it, for I'm sure there was a town named Freeport at one time. I never expected any difficulty, but by the time I came way out here I found no one had ever heard of it."

"Is it really important to you that you find it, or is it just a matter of curiosity?"

He thought that her face suddenly sobered. "I feel that it's awfully important, Ted. I don't mean in the way of money, or anything like that. My grandparents did own some property in Freeport, but I suppose that's all been disposed of. No, I want it for a reason which seems to me much more important than that. What I want most is to find out who I am."

"Who you are?" asked Ted, puzzled. "You're Nancy Lindell, aren't you?"

"Yes, that's my name. But what's a name, after all? Two people might have the same name, and yet they'd be altogether different persons. What I want most is to find out what sort of person I am."

"And you think finding Freeport would help you?"

"Yes." She hesitated a moment, then went on, "Perhaps you didn't know it, Ted, but my mother and father died when I was very small. I can hardly remember them now. I've never known my family at all."

"You've known your aunt," he pointed out.

"Yes, although she isn't really my aunt. She's a second cousin, and she knows very little about my family. Especially, she doesn't know anything about Freeport, or my grandmother, the mayor, for they are on opposite sides of my family."

"Supposing you did find Freeport, Nancy—then what?"

"Well, I'd try to find out more about my grandmother, and perhaps about my father when he was a little boy. I don't know whether I can make you understand, Ted, but it seems to me something like this. A person tends to become what the people around him want him to become. If I had been raised by my father and mother, then they would have brought me up in a certain way, and I would have become a certain kind of person. But that didn't happen to me. I don't know what sort of persons they were, or what they would have expected of me. Until I know that, I won't know just what sort of person they would have wanted me to be. Does this sound awfully silly, Ted?"

"No, I don't think so, Nancy," he said musingly. "You mean, if your parents had lived, you might have become a different sort of person than you are now. And you'd sort of like to find out what this different person would have been like, and perhaps become more like that person yourself."

"That's it, Ted. And if I could find out before I went to college, I think it might help me to decide which way I want to point my life, what I want to do and to become."

"Will you let me help you, Nancy?"

"Help me in what way, Ted?"

"Well, why don't we have lunch together tomorrow, and then stop at the library and see what we can find out about your Freeport? Maybe it won't be so hard after all."

"That sounds interesting, Ted. Let's do it. And thank you for a wonderful evening. Margaret isn't angry with me, is she?"

"Oh, no, not at all."

"I'm glad, because she's an awfully nice girl, Ted, and I know you've been friends for a long time. Good night."

"Good night, Nancy." He waited till she was upstairs, and he saw brighter lights flash on in the apartment overhead.

CHAPTER 10

PURPLE MONDAY

Shortly after noon on Monday, having had lunch at the restaurant, Ted and Nancy visited the library. Having explained their mission to the librarian, she gave them a huge volume that listed all the cities, towns, and villages in the entire state. They immediately turned to the F's, but running down the list soon determined that Freeport was not listed.

"There's a Fremont," Ted observed, "but that's as close as we can come."

Nancy looked disappointed, but was not prepared to give up. "It's just possible that the name has been changed, or the town annexed to a larger city, since my grandmother's day. Is there any way we can check on that?"

They discovered that whenever such a thing occurred, the old name or names were listed in parentheses after the present name. There seemed to be no way to discover these older names except by going through the entire list. It was a long job, consuming most of the remainder of their lunch hour, and when it was finished they were no nearer to their goal than they had been before.

"I can't understand it," said Nancy thoughtfully. "I'm certain there was a town of Freeport, even though there seems to be no re-cord of it now. From the way my grandmother described it, it must have had several thousand people. And there was a town square, and a village hall and fire wagon, and she mentioned a waterfall above the town." She considered for a few moments. "I wonder if Freeport could be a ghost town—someplace where people used to live but everyone has now moved away for some reason or other."

Ted grinned. "If it was a ghost town, it's probably disappeared by now. The tourists would have carried it away piece by piece. We can easily check on that, though. I remember seeing a book about all the ghost towns in the state."

He found the volume he was looking for without much trouble, and they went through it rapidly. There were only half-a-dozen hamlets which could be considered ghost towns by any stretch of the imagination, and none of these fitted the bill. None had been named Freeport, nor did any of them seem large enough to have a mayor.

"Well, we really didn't get anywhere," Ted decided as they left the library.

"At least we know a few things that *won't* help us," Nancy pointed out, "and sometimes that can be a big help. It does seem silly to believe a person could have lost a whole town, doesn't it?"

"Especially one as large as this," Ted decided. "Well, we won't give up on it entirely. I'll ask around among some old-timers, just to see if they can remember anything about Freeport. Maybe something will turn up."

After leaving Nancy, it occurred to Ted that it might be amusing to put an ad in the *Town Crier:* "Lost, one town, name of Freeport, believed to have been governed by a woman mayor. Will finder please advise the *Town Crier.* No personal questions will be asked."

Silly, of course, but a newspaper item just might turn the trick, if their other resources failed.

Ted was seeing less than usual of Mr. Woodring these dap. He rushed around from one appointment to another, and the stamp plan seemed to be catching fire. Ted had seen him only briefly that morning, but late in the afternoon Mr. Woodring came in. It was just a little early, and he seemed to have a little time to spare.

"Well, what have you been doing with yourself, Ted?" he asked, for they had become more friendly in the last few days.

"Oh, we had a hayride Saturday night," Ted explained. "Nancy— you remember her—claims that there is—or was—a town named Freeport in this state, but no one ever heard of it. Did you, by any chance?"

"No, I don't think so, though I'm not very well acquainted in this state. I know a Fremont, of course."

"No, she says it isn't Fremont. Well, I'm planning on asking some of the older residents."

"How did the young people like the stamps?" asked Mr. Woodring, changing the subject.

"Oh, I guess they like them all right. Most of the boys make fun of them, but then I guess boys don't do very much shopping any-way—not enough to bother saving stamps. They did kind of tease me about the stamps, though."

"What about them?" asked Mr. Woodring, alert to any possible criticism of the stamp plan which might affect their business adverse-ly.

"Just the color of the stamps. Everybody else says they're blue, but they look sort of purple to me. So of course that started them kid-ding me about the purple cow."

Mr. Woodring seemed to have pricked up his ears. "What makes you think the stamps are purple?"

"Oh—I don't know. Don't they look a little bit purple to you?"

"Of course not." He was probably speaking more harshly than he intended. "They look like a pure blue to me."

Ted could see that Mr. Woodring was upset and he tried to smooth things over. "Oh, well, maybe I was just expecting too much. I hope you don't think I've been shooting off my mouth. I certainly didn't want to do anything to hurt the stamp plan, and I don't think I did. It's just the way a young crowd gets to kidding around."

"I understand." But Mr. Woodring acted as though he didn't un-derstand, and his thoughts might have been a hundred miles away. He hardly said good night as Ted packed, up his few things and left for the night.

Ted's earlier doubts about the color of the stamps had almost disappeared but now he began to wonder. If Mr. Woodring was upset about this talk about a purple cow…did he really have anything to get upset about? The matter remained on his mind during supper and afterward as he tried to settle down to the evening paper. Why did those stamps look purplish to him and to Nancy, while they looked normal to everyone else? It didn't seem possible that the two of them had suddenly become color blind. Surely there must have been some-thing in their past experience, some conditioning influence, which led them to regard those stamps in a different light than other people did. What was different about Nancy and him? Then, suddenly, he had it, and sat bolt upright. That was it, of course! He almost ran to the telephone to put through a call to Nelson.

"Say, Nel, can you come over right away?"

"Sure. But what's up, Ted? You sound excited."

"Something about those stamps. Don't say anything to anybody else. I'll explain it to you when you get here."

His voice must have sounded urgent because Nelson drove up hardly five minutes later.

"O.K., Ted, let's have it. You've got me almost jumping out of my skin with curiosity."

They sat down on the swing, and Ted began with an air of suppressed excitement:

"You say these stamps still look blue to you, don't you?"

"Yes, and they look purple to you, don't they?"

"Well, purplish, anyway. Now what makes you think they're blue? You're comparing them with other blues you have known in the past, and they seem all right to you and almost everybody in town. But they don't look right to Nancy and to me. Now why don't they?"

"I'll bite."

"Because Nancy and I are comparing them with something else. We saw *different* stamps, and we know that these aren't the same. The others were a pure blue, just like those on the posters at the office."

"Where did you see these other stamps?" asked Nelson.

"At the *Town Crier* office, the day Mr. Woodring first came in to talk about his plan."

"Did anybody else see them?"

"I'm trying to think. Mr. Dobson passed them over to us, but he didn't have his reading glasses on, so I don't think he paid any attention to them. Carl Allison wasn't in, and Miss Monroe came in just as Mr. Woodring was leaving, so she didn't see them either."

"You don't have any samples of those other stamps now?"

"No, Mr. Woodring took them back. The only stamps anyone else has seen are the ones the stores have put in circulation, mostly Kirtland's. And those stamps are all more purple than the old stamps."

Suddenly Nelson began to grasp what Ted was driving at. "Hey, Ted, you think maybe these new stamps are counterfeits?"

"Blazes, I don't know. Let's try to figure out if they could be. Trading stamps aren't quite the same as money. You know how it is with currency or coins. Hardly anybody could tell you where he got every bill or every coin he's carrying around with him, and just in case he could, the person he got the bill from probably couldn't tell you where *he* got it. Money circulates so rapidly and through so many hands that if you try to trace a counterfeit bill it isn't going to be very long before you lose track of it. Even if you do find the counterfeiter, he could claim to be just an innocent party.

"Stamps are different. People hardly ever pass them around from one to the other. The Blue Harvest company distributes them to their salesmen, the salesmen sell them to the stores, the stores give them to their customers, and the customers turn them back to the Blue Harvest company for redemption. That means there aren't very many people involved, and that most people *will* know where they got their stamps."

"Well, supposing these stamps are counterfeits, who's responsible?"

"Let's work it out. It couldn't be Kirtland's and the other stores. Apparently they've *all* got the purple stamps. And I don't see how it could be the Blue Harvest company. After all, they print the stamps. Anything they say *is* good, *is* good. They could print any kind of stamp they want, as long as they're willing to redeem it. Of course they could print some stamps and later claim they were counterfeit so they wouldn't have to redeem them afterward. But by the time they tried that the whole stamp plan would collapse, and I don't think that's what they want. They're trying to build up confidence in these stamps, so they can stay in business for a long time."

"So that leaves—" said Nelson meaningfully.

"Yes," said Ted with deep regret, "that leaves nobody else but Mr. Woodring. If these stamps are counterfeit, he'd *have* to be responsible. There just isn't anybody else available."

"But what would he have to gain from it, Ted?"

"Well, I suppose there must be some way for him to make money on the deal. I imagine, when he turns over a batch of stamps to Kirtland's, the store pays him for the stamps, and then he has to account back to his company for the stamps he has sold. But if he sold Kirtland's some phony stamps he'd printed himself, he could just put the money in his pocket, and the Blue Harvest company wouldn't know the difference."

"But when people began to turn these stamps in for redemption, wouldn't Blue Harvest know then?"

"Maybe not. Maybe Mr. Woodring hoped that the counterfeits were so good that the Blue Harvest company wouldn't notice the difference. It turned out that they weren't that good, and that's what led to his trouble."

"But even supposing, Ted, that the counterfeits were very good imitations, wouldn't the Blue Harvest company soon notice they were getting more stamps back than they were giving out?"

"I suppose so, but maybe that would take quite a few months. Mr. Woodring could plan on pulling out before then."

Suddenly Nelson pounded his hand into his fist. "Maybe there's another way for Mr. Woodring to make money, Ted—a *lot* of money. There are lots of different kinds of trading stamps, and the business must be awfully competitive. Maybe one of these other companies hired Mr. Woodring to put fake Blue Harvest stamps into circulation, in order to discredit the Blue Harvest company and send them out of business."

"That may be. Oh, I suppose there are lots of ways an unscrupulous person could make money on a deal like this. For example—I don't think this really happened, but it's just a possibility—one of the North Ridge stores could have hired Mr. Woodring to discredit the Blue Harvest stamps. Only one thing really bothers me. These stamps *are* different. If anybody saw both the old and the new stamps, he'd notice the difference right off. Would Mr. Woodring be able to take a chance like that? At least he'd want counterfeits that were good enough so he wouldn't get tripped up right away."

"Don't you see, Ted, it *has* to be that way," Nelson pointed out. "These counterfeits *had* to be poor, so that the difference *would* be quickly noticed. That would be the only way the stamps could be easily discredited."

"Yes, that may be right. But if so, then Mr. Woodring wouldn't be planning on hanging around very long. As soon as he knew he'd worked all the damage he could, he'd light out. Oh, oh, I just thought of something terrible!"

"What?"

"I got to talking with Mr. Woodring today about the purple cow. He knows now that the difference has been spotted. He became awfully subdued and distant after I said that. He may think the alarm is out by now. If he's going to leave town, tonight would be just about the best time for it. Well, what can we do? Is there any way to stop him?"

"Whoa, Ted, wait a minute, cool off," Nelson cautioned him. "We still don't know for *sure* that these stamps are counterfeit. You say the colors are different. O.K., so far. But still that doesn't necessarily make them counterfeit. You were speaking about United States currency a little while ago, and we know how carefully that's printed and safeguarded. But stamps aren't currency, and I don't think they're printed that carefully. I feel pretty sure a much less expensive process is used. It could be that the Blue Harvest company did issue some stamps which were a little different. Maybe something happened to go a little bit wrong with the ink in their print shop. Maybe they deliberately decided to change the color of their stamps for some reason or other. That still doesn't make the stamps counterfeit."

"Then how could we tell?"

"I suppose the only way to tell for sure would be to have a representative of the Blue Harvest company look at these stamps and decide whether they're good or not."

"What representative? Mr. Woodring is the only representative they've got out here."

"Well, it would have to be somebody besides Mr. Woodring, of course. Maybe the company could fly out a representative tomorrow, if Mr. Dobson asked them quietly."

Ted groaned. "Now you've got me all mixed up. Now that I think back over everything, I feel almost positive these stamps are phonies. But I can see, too, that nobody except someone from the Blue Harvest company can prove it, and meanwhile we have to go easy. If we create suspicion over these stamps, then we'll be causing all the damage ourselves that we suspect Mr. Woodring of trying to cause. I suppose I'll have to tell Mr. Dobson about it, but while all this is going on Mr. Woodring will have flown the coop. Wait a minute—I think I'm going to call him at the hotel."

"Why?" Nelson demanded.

"Just to see if he's still there. If he is, maybe we can stop him from leaving. I'll make up some excuse for calling him. Maybe tell him Mr. Dobson wants to see him about some more publicity for the plan. If he answers, I'll have to call Mr. Dobson about it fast."

Ted jumped up and hurried inside and put through his call. The desk was unable to put him through to Mr. Woodring's room.

"I'm sorry, Ted," the clerk told him, "but Mr. Woodring told me that he would be in Peninsula this evening, and I should take his calls for him. Any message?"

"No, I guess not. It can wait till morning."

Back on the front porch, Ted reported to Nelson.

"Then he did beat it," Nelson commented.

"No, maybe not. I remember now, he really did have an appointment in Peninsula for this evening. So I guess I won't know for sure until tomorrow whether he's really gone. That's what gripes me. Here, while I'm doing nothing, he's likely to make a clean getaway."

"Well, what's the difference?" asked Nelson.

"What do you mean?"

"Suppose he does get away, what harm is it going to do? He hasn't had a chance to put very many of these counterfeits into circulation. Oh, maybe the Blue Harvest company will lose a few thousand dollars, but I guess they can afford it. Anyway, a new company always expects to take some losses before they get established. The real harm is the damage Mr. Woodring's been able to do to the stamp plan, and he's done all that already. He won't be able to do anything more between now and morning."

"I guess you're right," said Ted slowly. "And of course it's possible that we're barking up the wrong tree. The stamps *could* be genuine. We won't know for sure, until we see whether Mr. Woodring shows up tomorrow morning or not."

"Sure, Ted, just assume that everything's all right, and get a good night's sleep. Tomorrow always comes soon enough, anyway."

And while Ted tried to follow this advice, thinking back over Mr. Woodring's strange preoccupation that afternoon, he knew with an ache in his heart that he wasn't going to show up the next morning.

CHAPTER 11

THE LOCKED DOOR

Fifteen minutes before opening time Ted was cooling his heels, pacing up and down in front of the office, hoping but not really expecting that Mr. Woodring would show up. Opening time came and went, and still the door of the office was firmly locked. He determined to wait half an hour longer, just to give Mr. Woodring the benefit of the doubt. When this half-hour, too, had passed, he knew what he had to do.

He went across to the drugstore and telephoned the hotel. He asked for Mr. Woodring's room, but after the phone had rung eight or ten times with no response, the desk clerk came on.

"I'm sorry, but there's no answer. Can I take a message?"

"This is Ted Wilford, and I've been working for Mr. Woodring. It's very important that I reach him. Can you send up a messenger to see if he's there?"

"All right, Ted, I'll try it."

Ted hung on a few minutes longer before the clerk came on again. "Mr. Woodring isn't here. It looks as though he's left, bag and baggage."

"Didn't he check out?"

"No, he's still listed on the register. He hasn't turned in his key."

"Did he pay for his room?"

"Yes, he was paid up for the rest of this week. I suppose we'll have to keep the room available for him, just in case he does come back, but if a guest intends to return he doesn't usually take every single item with him. Well, if he doesn't come back, all we're out is a key, but we don't like to do business that way."

Ted thanked him and hung up. There could no longer be the slightest doubt that Mr. Woodring had taken flight—taken it because of what Ted had said yesterday about the purple cow. This left Ted with no alternative but to report the matter to Mr. Dobson, who was, after all, his real employer.

At the *Town Crier* office Ted told Mr. Dobson exactly what had happened. Miss Monroe and Nancy were there, too, and they also listened to his story. The editor's face was very sober as Ted concluded.

"I suppose it was my fault," Ted decided. "If I had really thought there was anything wrong about those stamps, I should have told you about it, instead of Mr. Woodring. This gave him a chance to get away. But up until last night I thought this whole purple-cow business could be explained somehow."

"Don't blame yourself, Ted," the editor admonished him. "It was my fault entirely. We had plenty of opportunity to realize something was wrong. You told me Mr. Woodring had been lying about the 3 percent. I found he had never worked at Beacon, Jones and Western, as he claimed. Nancy mentioned something to me yesterday about purple cows, but Monday's our deadline morning, and I didn't pay much attention. I can see now that I've been frightfully careless. I still believe the company is honest—I checked into them pretty thoroughly—but I didn't think to check more closely into their salesman, or to believe what I found when I did. I was so anxious to come up with some plan that would revive our slipping business that I jumped in too fast. There's no one to blame except myself."

"And Mr. Woodring," Ted added.

"Well, I suppose we'd better figure out something. I imagine the best thing to do would be to notify the Blue Harvest company and see what they want to do about it. That might be better than alarming Mr. Kirtland and the others before we know exactly where we stand. I'll put the call through right now."

Within a couple of minutes he was speaking with an officer of Blue Harvest by long distance. Just what the officer promised wasn't clear to the other listeners until after the editor hung up. He explained to them:

"They'll have a man out here by four o'clock this afternoon. They're as much surprised and upset about it as we are. Something like this could wreck their whole operation. Ted, can you be here this afternoon? You might be able to tell them more about this matter than I can."

"Yes, I'll be here," he promised.

There was no reason why Ted couldn't have hung around the office if he wanted to. This had been his custom in the old days—just getting his nose full of printer's ink and helping out with any little tasks that might come up. But Carl Allison came in just then. He had a few words with Mr. Dobson, then, finding he couldn't ignore Ted's presence any longer, said a brief "Hello, Ted," and turned away to his typewriter. It was about this time that Ted decided the office was getting too crowded, and drifted on toward home.

He passed the Blue Harvest office just as a matter of curiosity, and found the door still locked. As he stood there for a few moments, the telephone began to ring inside. He felt it was his duty to answer, but there was no way for him to manage it short of breaking in, and presently the ringing stopped. He walked on toward home, surprising his mother by his early appearance and his tale of what had taken place.

The day dragged on. Ted put through a call to Nelson to tell him what had happened, though he asked him to keep it quiet at least until the end of the day. Nelson was hardly surprised by this development, but all he could do was offer some unhelpful sympathy. They soon hung up, and Ted returned to his moping.

He was back at the *Town Crier* office before four o'clock. The man from Blue Harvest arrived at about the expected time and introduced himself as Mr. Bentley. He was gray-haired and bespectacled, and had very thin lips which he kept tightly clenched, betraying his tension.

"You have no idea where Mr. Woodring is now?" This was his first question to Ted, and Ted replied in the negative.

"He was supposed to have an appointment in Peninsula last night. I don't know whether he kept it or not."

"I'll check on that as soon as I can. He didn't drop any hint of where he might have gone?"

Ted shook his head.

"No, I don't suppose he would. We've done a little more checking on Mr. Woodring since your call this morning, Mr. Dobson. We find that, far from working for Beacon, Jones and Western ten years ago, he was in prison at the time. Convicted for embezzlement, I might add. I don't say we wouldn't have employed him had we known, because many a man who has gone wrong once is deserving of another chance, but at least we would have watched him more closely."

In prison! Somehow the idea had never occurred to Ted. But now he remembered Mr. Woodring saying that he used to do a great deal of reading when he had more time. He must have meant while he was in prison. What had seemed a simple, careless statement had had a deeper significance, if Ted had only been able to spot it.

"Mr. Woodring made some representation that your stamps were redeemable at 3 percent," Mr. Dobson advised him. "Is this a company policy, by any chance?"

"Certainly not," Mr. Bentley snapped. "We sell our stamps at 2 percent, and we redeem them at 2 percent—and give excellent value for the money, I must say. But it is 2 percent, and we've never authorized our salesmen to say anything else. Instead, we ask them not to stress the percentage at all, but rather to concentrate on the high quality of our luxury products. I wish we could give 3 percent for 2 percent, but I don't know how to do it and still stay in business."

"It seems to me," Mr. Dobson pursued, "that the whole crux of the matter is whether or not these so-called purple-cow stamps are genuine or not. I imagine that you may not have seen them as yet, Mr. Bentley. Would you care to take a look at them and express an opinion?"

He handed the visitor a sheet of stamps. Upon looking at them, Mr. Bentley seemed startled, and then he studied them very closely for a few minutes. It appeared that he wasn't so much looking at the stamps as trying to make up his mind about something. At last his decision was made, and he looked up.

"These stamps are perfectly genuine," he announced. "It is true they are slightly more purplish than most of our stamps, but that can easily be explained by a slight difference in the mixing of the ink in our printing office."

"Now just a moment, Mr. Bentley," the editor interposed. "The entire situation indicates that these stamps are counterfeits. Now if—"

"I said they are genuine," the other interrupted, "and as long as my company accepts them as genuine, then they are genuine."

"You're making this very difficult," said Mr. Dobson, somewhat annoyed. "If you say these stamps are genuine, then I don't see that you have any fault to find at all with Mr. Woodring. Without pressing charges, you can't expect to enlist the help of the police."

"He may have run off with some company money," said Mr. Bentley stiffly, "or at least he hasn't rendered us an accounting, as we rightfully expected from him. I feel sure the police will be prepared to help us on that basis."

"Did he really get away with very much money?" asked Ted, as the men paused and almost glared at each other.

"I don't have any figures as yet, of course. We work our salesmen on a bonus plan. Our general policy is to give them a bonus for opening a new account. This amounts to the value of the stamps which the business would normally use in a month—based upon average of the previous year's sales. Of course, Mr. Woodring may have unloaded more than a month's supply of stamps on some of the businesses and pocketed the money. Our loss will come when we are required to redeem the stamps which will eventually be turned in."

"Then if Mr. Woodring ran off with the receipts which the companies gave to him, it would be mostly his own money anyway, wouldn't it?"

"Possibly, although he owed us an accounting of it, at least. I can see that we shall have to change company policy in that respect and not permit the salesmen to handle these receipts directly and in their own names. In the future, checks will be sent directly to the company. But I'm not so much concerned with the direct monetary loss Mr. Woodring has caused us as the damage he may have done to the entire stamp plan."

"How large was Mr. Woodring's territory?" asked Ted. "He seemed to be traveling over quite a large area."

"He held the territory from here to the state line. We have another man in Johnston City, across the state border. Both offices were opened at the same time, and our salesmen came out together."

"Now about these purple stamps, what does your company intend to do about them?" Mr. Dobson questioned.

"Those that have found their way into the hands of customers we shall redeem, of course, when they are turned in. For those stamps which the stores are holding I shall have them replaced with genuine—that is to say, stamps about which there can't be any question."

"Then you are admitting that these purple stamps are counterfeits?"

"I'm admitting nothing of the sort! I'm simply saying that the public may not have full confidence in them, and therefore it would be better to replace them. The mistake should have been caught in our own printing office, but unfortunately must have slipped by."

"Can you be sure from your brief examination of these stamps, Mr. Bentley, that these stamps are actually genuine?"

"I'm quite sure that they are. They could have come from nowhere except Mr. Woodring, and he could have gotten them from nowhere except our own office."

"Isn't it possible he could have counterfeited them?"

"I doubt it. In the first place, I can't see why he should, since it is the kind of fraud which couldn't pay him very much and at which he would very soon be caught. But real or phony makes no difference. My company will redeem them, and so that makes them real. Now I have a question for you, Mr. Dobson. I realize you are a newspaperman, and I know something of your reputation. Just what do you intend to do about this story?"

"What do you propose that I do about it?" the editor countered.

"I can't see any reason why it should ever go beyond these four walls. I'm sure we are all discreet persons here. Besides, I can't see that there is any story at all, as long as my company redeems the stamps."

The editor slowly shook his head. "I've never yet covered up a news story because it was profitable for me to do so, and I don't propose to begin this late in the game. But even if I wanted to, I don't think I could. The rumors are around already. A police report on Mr. Woodring will spread the rumors further—"

"I'm not sure that there need be a police report on Mr. Woodring, after all. If he's made his getaway, I'm almost inclined to say good riddance."

"But the thing that will give the whole thing away is that you are going to put the blue Blue Harvest stamps back into circulation. So far only Ted and Nancy have noticed the difference. But as soon as the other stamps begin circulating, other people will spot it, too, and will have questions to ask."

Mr. Bentley pursed his lips but said nothing, and Mr. Dobson went on:

"I think the best thing you can do, Mr. Bentley, is to prepare a statement for publication. I shall, of course, be glad to print your statement in my story on the subject."

"Then I can give you my statement right now. 'Due to an unfortunate error at our printing office, a few of our stamps are of a slightly more purple shade than some of the others. This, however, should not be a matter of concern. All the stamps are perfectly genuine, and my company shall be very happy to redeem them for premiums as listed in our fine catalogue.'"

"All right, Mr. Bentley," said Mr. Dobson, a little skeptically, "if that's your story, I hope that you are able to make it stick. And as long as you insist they're genuine, it would be pretty difficult for anyone else to prove they're not. I only hope Mr. Woodring doesn't have you in so deep that you'll find further difficulties coming up."

After Mr. Bentley had left, Mr. Dobson expressed something more of his doubts to Ted.

"I wish this thing could blow over as simply as Mr. Bentley would like to believe, but I'm afraid there are going to be repercussions. For one thing, there's Mr. Woodring's car—it's a company car, and ought to be reported stolen. If it turns up without being reported, there will be some questions from the police. Then there are the checks Mr. Woodring is holding. Some of these are probably company checks, and he may forge the endorsements. And he may have made other contracts and commitments, all in the company's name, that will be difficult to fulfill. I'm very much afraid the full extent of his wrongdoing hasn't yet been uncovered."

"Will this leave the *Town Crier* in the clear?" asked Ted.

"Not so clear as I should like it, Ted, since we helped sponsor the stamp plan in the first place. But if Mr. Bentley thinks I will give him any help at all in covering up matters from here on, he's very much mistaken. And I may say a few things he won't like at all, such as emphasizing the 2 percent aspect of the deal and explaining the background of the plan. Some of these stamp companies would like to make people believe they really are getting something for nothing, but it isn't quite like that. I intend to go into the subject pretty thoroughly, including some comments from people on both sides of the matter."

As Ted left the office he had rather a letdown feeling. He was now unemployed, and although he might enjoy his two weeks of freedom, still he had the feeling that things were going on in which he had no part. He no longer worked for Blue Harvest. Whatever was going to be done about the matter was out of his hands. He explained all this to Nelson that evening.

"Well, we've still got Farmer Smith's purple cow, Ted. Why don't we take a ride out and see just what the gimmick is?"

CHAPTER 12

MR. SMITH'S COW

The farmer was busy with chores at the moment they arrived, and Mrs. Smith suggested that they wait for him out by the pasture fence.

"Then he really does have a purple cow?" asked Ted with a skeptical smile.

She smiled in return. "I guess it's mostly in how you look at things. It's his story, so I'd better not spoil it for him."

They waited at the place indicated, and some fifteen minutes later Mr. Smith came sauntering up to them.

"Come out to see my purple cow, did you, boys?" he asked cheerfully. "Well, that won't take long. There she is, yonder in the pasture. What do you think?"

Turning in the direction indicated, they saw a lone cow munching grass on a hillside. She had been there all along, but they had given her no attention, for there certainly was nothing at all remarkable about her coloring. It was an ordinary white cow, with some dark markings.

"Is that all?" asked Ted in disappointment, having somehow hoped for more than this.

"It looks like just a white cow to me," said Nelson firmly.

"Well, now, let's not be too hasty about this," the farmer suggested. "You say it's white. But this is daytime, you know, even if it is getting on toward sunset. Suppose it was pitch black outside, then what color would the cow be?"

"It'd still be white," replied Nelson with conviction. "A white cow is a white cow, day or night."

But Ted was beginning to catch the farmer's drift and was picking up interest. "I suppose if the night were dark enough, the cow would be black, and we wouldn't be able to see it at all."

The farmer nodded in agreement. "That's right. Now suppose it were night, but there was just a little light, so that you could see the cow. Then what color would the cow be?"

"I suppose it would be white," said Ted, a little doubtfully.

"Yes, you'd call it white, but that's because you *knew* it was white. If you didn't know that, you might not be sure of its color at all. And even if you said it *is* white, would it be the same white that you'd see in the daytime?"

"No," Nelson returned, "because there wouldn't be enough light to see it by."

"That's quite correct. So then you'd have to admit that my cow does change color sometime during the day. Maybe I could make it clearer by talking about a red book. In the daylight it looks bright red. In the dark it looks simply black. Then the book must have changed color, from red to black, at some time or other. Now when did it change—all in a moment? No, it changed gradually, as the light was changing. And we all know when the light changes the most—at twilight. Look at my cow again—look carefully—and tell me what color you *really* think she looks like."

Once more they studied the cow carefully. It was a very strange thing, because they *knew* that the cow was white. But the sun was now close to the horizon, shadows were lengthening, and the light was gradually fading from the sky. And the cow *did* look a little different. The color was no longer the bright white they would have seen during the day. Was there—could there be—just a shade of purple in the cow's tint?

"Holy mackerel!" exclaimed Nelson. "Call me crazy if you want to, but I'm beginning to think that cow's *purple!*"

"That's right," the farmer agreed. "We're so used to seeing things the way we know them to be that very often we fail to see how they really look. I don't think there's anything so strange about a purple cow, after all, if you consider the way a cow and everything else change color at twilight. The trouble is, most of the time it takes an artist to point these things out to us. And then, just as likely as not, people will say the artist is crazy, and go right on calling the cow white, when it actually looks purple."

"But the cow really *is* white," Nelson observed. "You've got to admit that."

"No, I don't think I'm prepared to admit that," said the farmer cautiously. "Let's say the cow is white in the daytime, purple at twilight, and black at night. Why should we say that the daytime color is any more real than the twilight color, or the nighttime color?"

This was an interesting viewpoint, even though they weren't quite prepared to accept the underlying philosophy. After all, Gelett Burgess claimed that he had never seen a purple cow, and millions of other people all agreed with him, didn't they?

As Ted turned away, some of his disappointment returned to him. This had been an interesting experiment, but something rather less than he had expected. It appeared to have nothing at all to do with the matter of the purple-cow stamps which had been weighing so heavily on his mind.

He began to thank the farmer, preparatory to taking their leave, but Mr. Smith interrupted him.

"Oh, I'm not finished yet, Ted. I did have a particular reason for asking *you* to come out. I've got something to show you, but I don't know whether you would have believed it, if you hadn't seen my cow in the pasture first. Come on up to the house for a few minutes."

They followed the farmer up the path and into the house, where he led them into the living room and switched on a light.

"There." He motioned toward the opposite wall. "I told you I had a purple cow, and this one's purple all the time."

"A cow in the house?" Nelson muttered to himself, before realizing that the farmer was referring to a painting on the wall.

It was a very attractive painting, they quickly realized. It was a pastoral scene, with a cow strolling past a fence on a country lane. Most startling was the fact, if a person stopped to think about it, that the cow was a vivid purple. But taken in the setting of the picture, the cow did not look strange at all. The viewer assumed that the scene occurred at twilight and that the coloring of the cow was perfectly appropriate under the circumstances.

"Boy, Gelett Burgess should have seen this," Nelson exclaimed. "What's the name of the picture?"

"Oh, it has some very formal name—*A Study at Twilight,* or something like that. But nobody ever calls it by that name. It's popularly called *The Purple Cow.*"

"Isn't that a valuable painting?" Ted inquired.

"It would be," said the farmer regretfully, "if it were an original. Unfortunately, it's only a copy. But it's a *good* copy—hand drawn. There are only a few of them, and lots of people come out to see my painting. The original, by Jan Fountaine, hangs in a museum. They've got some rather strict rules about photographing it, and things like that. I had a fellow come out here only a few months ago, to ask me to allow him to take a picture of this."

"Did you?" asked Nelson.

"Sure. Why not? If he's breaking the copyright laws, or anything like that, it's his lookout, not mine. Well, Ted, what do you think of my purple cow?"

"It's a very nice picture, I guess, but… Say, wait a minute!" Ted was growing excited once more. "This picture is beginning to look awfully familiar."

"Is it?" Mr. Smith chuckled. "I was wondering how long it would take you to catch on."

"Catch on to what?" Nelson demanded. "I don't see anything the matter with it."

"Don't you?" asked Ted, almost elatedly. "Look at the way that tree overhangs, and the barn, and the hills in the background."

"Wait a minute, wait a minute. Now I'm beginning to get it. Hey, could this be the same picture that's on those Blue Harvest stamps?"

"Guess it is," the farmer admitted, grinning broadly. "I thought Ted would be interested in that."

"I sure am," Ted agreed. He studied the picture once more. The similarity was apparent once you stopped to think about it, but it wasn't so clear at first glance. There were matters of size and brush stroking. Then the picture had been somewhat trimmed around the edges for purposes of fitting it on the stamp without reducing the size excessively. And there was color, for while the painting consisted of many brilliant hues, all, these had been reduced to just one color on the stamps, a blue—or purple.

"What about this fellow who took the picture—the picture of the painting?" Ted questioned. "What did he look like?"

"I don't exactly remember." The farmer looked vague. "You see, I get quite a number of visitors to see my painting. And I was pretty busy at the time, too. I remember, I'd just had a telephone call that the milk truck had broken down and—"

"Can't you remember anything about him?" Ted pressed him.

"Well, let me see, I think he was just an ordinary-looking fellow. I remember he wore a raincoat and hat, because it had been raining pretty heavily that day. I guess he was about thirty, average height, well built. And his hair was black—I think. Oh, one more thing. I remember he was left-handed, because he gave me a few dollars for letting him take the picture, and I recall he reached into his left-hand pocket for it."

"Oh." The description was certainly vague enough, and could fit thousands of men. "I was wishing he'd given you his name."

"Oh, but he did give me his name! It was Winthrop—Mr. Winthrop. Yes, I remember that now, because my second cousin's daughter married a man—"

"Well, I guess that's that." Ted's voice sounded very dejected. "Thanks very much, Mr. Smith. It was worth the trip out here to see your painting."

"That's what they all tell me," said Mr. Smith, pleased. He offered them refreshments as they passed by the kitchen door, but they declined with thanks, and calling a good-by to him and his wife, they set out for home.

"What's with the name Winthrop, Ted?" asked Nelson, turning the car into the highway. "You acted like you recognized it. It was just a phony, wasn't it?"

"Yes, and not even a very good phony. That's Mr. Woodring's first name—Winthrop Woodring. The description fits him, too. Well, that just goes to prove that he had this whole thing planned out months ago."

"You knew that already, didn't you? He couldn't have printed those fake stamps overnight."

"I know, but I guess I just didn't want to admit it. This is not the case of a man suddenly going wrong. It was a long, carefully thought-out plan. And not a very good plan, either, since he wouldn't be able to dispose of very many of his fake stamps."

"How do you know that, Ted? He wouldn't necessarily have had to dispose of his stamps to stores, would he? Could he have sold them to individuals, say at half price, so they could turn them in for the premiums?"

"That's right, he could. But he'd have to sell them to the stores, too, I'd think. Say the stores all had genuine stamps, and certain individuals had fake stamps, this would point suspicion directly at them, and they'd have to tell where they got the stamps. But as long as the stores had fake stamps, too, then people could always claim they got them from the stores."

"So that's why he had to become a salesman for Blue Harvest," Nelson observed.

"I guess so. Well, I wish I knew where to put my hands on Mr. Woodring right now."

"Why, what good would it do?"

"I don't know exactly, but he sort of took us all in—Mr. Dobson, me, the whole town—and I don't like to see things end that way."

"Well, that's out of your hands. If the police can't find him, I don't think you can, either."

"That's just it. I doubt very much that Mr. Bentley intends to notify the police. He'd just like to say good riddance to Mr. Woodring once and for all. There's probably nothing he can do to get back the money Mr. Woodring stole, anyway."

"The Blue Harvest company will have to make good on those fake stamps, won't they? And how can they tell how many Mr. Woodring put into circulation?"

"They can't—but I guess they feel it doesn't matter very much. It couldn't be too many, and they'll have to make good no matter how many there are, so that people won't lose confidence in the stamps."

"What does Mr. Dobson think?"

"I guess he thinks the police ought to be notified. He doesn't believe you can get rid of Mr. Woodring and his work that easily. There's the stolen car, for instance—a company car. That's likely to turn up somewhere. Mr. Woodring wouldn't dare travel very far in a car the police were looking for."

"But the police *aren't* looking for it"

"Sure, but he doesn't know that. Oh, we've all been took—royally, and I'm beginning to get kind of burned about it. He had such a quiet, friendly air."

"Just like all confidence men," Nelson pointed out. "Anyway, I don't see how you could do anything about it. If he fooled Mr. Dobson, then all you could do was to follow Mr. Dobson's lead."

"Maybe, but if I'd only been a little more alert, maybe I would have known what he was up to. Yes, I'd like to meet Mr. Woodring again and give him a piece of my mind. After that he could go his own way, if Mr. Bentley doesn't want to enter charges."

"Didn't he give you any hint of where he might go, Ted? Did he talk about his family, or anything like that? You were the only one who was at all well acquainted with him."

"I don't think he had any family, at least he didn't mention any. There was one little thing, though. He said he had a cabin in the woods—a place he liked to go to spend his vacations."

"Did he tell you where it was?"

"No, but I kind of thought it was somewhere up north. He made a vague gesture over his shoulder, and we were traveling south at the time. Oh, one more thing—he said it overlooked two waterfalls. That ought to be some help."

"What's a waterfall?" Nelson snorted. "You can take a storm sewer sticking out of a hillside and call that a waterfall if you want to. Anyway, I never heard of two waterfalls close together. Did you?"

"No, not that I know of. Oh, I suppose it isn't any very big or very famous place. Maybe you're right. It could simply be two little trickles coming out of a hill."

"Maybe only one," Nelson decided. "One waterfall could be above his cabin, and one below it, all on the same stream."

"That's right, I suppose it could. Well, then, there probably wouldn't be anything very strange about that, and chances are we'll never find the place. I don't care very much, anyway. What's the use of seeing Mr. Woodring again? He wouldn't tell us anything, and I guess I wouldn't get very much pleasure shooting off my mouth at him, anyway. That's a pretty cheap kind of satisfaction, after all."

Nelson yawned. "Then that's the end of the purple cow?"

"I guess so—as far as I'm concerned. I'm just going to bed early tonight, and go to sleep and hope I don't dream about purple cows. And then I'm going to enjoy myself for the rest of my vacation."

"Alone?" asked Nelson wisely.

"Alone? Well, partly. And partly not. I just might decide to take a little whirl at finding Nancy's lost town for her."

"Sure." Nelson grinned. "It's a good thing she lost her town. It gives you a chance to pretend you're doing something for her."

"Oh, I don't think I'd need to pretend anything," Ted retorted.

CHAPTER 13

A LATE CALLER

There had been nothing in Tuesday's *Town Crier* about the crisis concerning the Blue Harvest stamps. On the contrary, there was an editorial drawing attention to the plan and expressing the hope that it would act to stimulate local trade. The paper's deadline was noon on Monday, and up to that time few facts were definitely known. It was not until Tuesday morning that Ted had told the editor of Mr. Woodring's alleged disappearance. Nor would Mr. Dobson have cared to print anything about the matter until he had talked with Mr. Bentley.

But there could be few doubts concerning the facts now, and Ted knew that there would be an article of some sort in the paper's next issue, on Friday morning. This would be a sad day for Mr. Dobson, and an uncomfortable one for all the merchants who had signed up for the plan. It wasn't going to do the plan any good to advertise the fact that a swindler had been connected with it. But it was hopeless to expect Mr. Dobson to pull in his horns, and Ted knew that he would print the article, exactly as he had promised.

Somehow Ted felt a growing sense of responsibility—a responsibility he had always felt where the newspaper was concerned. He was part of the Blue Harvest plan, too, and if it failed he felt that he would share in the failure. But more than that something Nelson had said stuck in his mind. It was true that Ted had been more friendly with Mr. Woodring than anybody else. If anyone was going to find him—and Ted was beginning to feel that finding him might serve a useful purpose, if Mr. Woodring could be made to explain the exact extent of the swindle and whether or not other people were involved—then perhaps it was up to him to do what he could. But a cabin between two waterfalls—even if Mr. Woodring had really gone there—sounded like an improbable place, and didn't suggest anything at all to Ted's mind. He did stop in at the library to see if he could find anything to help him, but found nothing new. Apparently the two waterfalls were as elusive as Nancy's mysteriously disappearing town.

At noon there was an item on the newscast mentioning Mr. Woodring's car. It was a last-minute item, and there were no details other than that the car had been found abandoned on a lonely road some twenty miles to the south, that it apparently had been driven by a Mr. Woodring of Forestdale, whom the police were unable to reach. The car had not been reported stolen. Ted could see that Mr. Dobson had been right. The police were in the case now, whether Mr. Bentley wanted it that way or not, and there were going to be all sorts of questions. It would be up to Mr. Bentley to provide the answers. Still, none of this seemed to concern Ted very directly. He felt he was on the outside, looking in.

Ted called up Nancy, but she had made herself quite popular at the hayride and was out on another date. Margaret, too, proved to be out. He decided to spend the evening reading, and his mother was busy in the kitchen, doing some baking for a charity bazaar the next day.

At ten o'clock the door chimes rang. Callers this late were unusual, and Ted put down his book with a feeling of curiosity as well as some worry. He hurried to open the door.

"Ted Wilford?" It was a man wearing a light overcoat, though the evening was warm.

"Yes," Ted admitted.

"I'm Mr. Dunfield from the Treasury Department, and I'd like to talk with you for a few minutes. May I come in?"

Ted studied the credentials the man had presented, then agreed. "Sure, come on in. But good gravy, what did we do now? Didn't we pay all our income tax?"

"Oh, yes—or at least I hope you did." The man smiled. "That's another branch of the department."

Ted led the way into the living room and invited him to sit down. He did, but got up at once as Mrs. Wilford came into the room.

"Mom, this is Mr. Dunfield from the Treasury Department. Mr. Dunfield, my mother." Ted explained quickly to his mother, "He says he isn't here about income tax."

"No, just a little matter I thought your son might be able to help me on," the government man put in quickly.

"In that case, I'm sure you gentlemen will excuse me," said Mrs. Wilford promptly. "I'm afraid I have some baking started."

She hurried from the room. Mr. Dunfield regarded her with approval, and Ted smiled. Although he knew that his mother was busy baking, he didn't think there was anything urgent about it that demanded her attention immediately. She left because she felt this was an affair of Ted's that he could handle competently for himself.

"I've come about this matter of the trading stamps, the Blue Harvest stamps," Mr. Dunfield began. He leaned back and crossed his legs.

Ted frowned. "I should have thought that was a little outside your field."

"Ordinarily, Ted, I suppose you might say it is. I'll tell you what I'm concerned about, and how I enter into the case. As you know, our government takes every possible precaution to insure that our currency is genuine. I can think of no domestic situation which would send this country into a panic as easily as the widespread belief that our currency, or any sizable portion of it, was phony. To avoid this possibility, the government must do all it can—not merely to punish counterfeiting—but to prevent it."

"You mean that there's a question of counterfeit currency in this case?" asked Ted with narrowing eyes.

"I don't *know* that there is, Ted, but we are faced with a certain combination of circumstances. We know there is some person who has the necessary skills to counterfeit our currency, and we know this man has an apparent background of antisocial behavior—by which I mean that he has served a prison sentence. This combination offers the possibility that Mr. Woodring *may* turn his talents to the counterfeiting of currency, and we must be alert to that possibility."

"Are you *sure* that these Blue Harvest stamps are counterfeits?" Ted asked of him.

"Oh, yes. There can be no question at all that the stamps circulating in Forestdale are counterfeits—no matter how much the company may choose to deny it. The quality of the paper is almost the same—so close that no one except an expert could tell the difference. But the color of the ink is of a distinctly different shade."

"Couldn't that have been a mistake in the print shop where the stamps were printed?"

"Possibly, Ted, but that's not all. If you were to examine these stamps under a magnifying lens—and compare them with the genuine stamps—you would be able to observe many tiny differences; that is, provided you knew what to look for. They are very skilled imitations, but they are imitations, nevertheless. I understand you've had some experience in the printing field, so you probably know how these stamps are printed. The pictures are engraved on metal plates, and then these metal plates are used to print the stamps. As I said, these plates were so well prepared that the suggestion of counterfeiting would probably never have arisen if it had not been for the obvious difference in the ink. That seems like a frightfully careless mistake for anyone to make. I suppose the criminal has a rather inflated idea of his own cunning—nearly all of them do—and that is what led him to circulate the stamps, in spite of the possibility they might arouse suspicion."

"Isn't it possible," Ted countered, "that he *wanted* the fraud to be discovered, in order to arouse public distrust of these trading stamps?"

The Treasury man seemed struck by the thought. "I admit that's a possibility which didn't occur to me. On the face of it, it doesn't appear very likely. These stamps are too easily traced. Most criminals prefer to act in the dark, and hope they won't be discovered. This type of operation means that the criminal would be known to a great many people, and his only hope of getting away with it would be to make his escape just before things got too hot for him. Still, given a certain type of criminal mind, and a great enough reward, it's possible he would do just that. The facts that the stamps were so clearly of a different color—seen as soon as anyone got around to making the direct comparison—and that Mr. Woodring *did* make his escape just before we caught up with him, offer the possibility that you may be right."

"I'm afraid I was the one who tipped him off," said Ted apologetically. "I remarked to him about the way the gang was joking over these purple-cow stamps. Of course I wasn't thinking about counterfeiting at the time."

"'Purple-cow' stamps? Well, that's a pretty good name for them. But I don't think you were responsible, Ted. This all adds up to a very shrewd operation, and I'm sure that Mr. Woodring must have been very much aware of what the score was. As a matter of fact, I've learned that he received a large check just yesterday afternoon, a few hours before he disappeared. I think it was that check which was the decisive factor. As soon as he had it, it was profitable for him to leave, and he did."

"How did you people get on to it so soon?" Ted questioned. "These stamps have only been in circulation for a few days."

"Oh, we have informants who give us tips on anything questionable which comes up in this line. Most of the tips are phonies, but we have to investigate them anyway, and once in a while one of them pans out. We had an inquiry about these stamps, based on the color of the ink. As you mentioned before, this could have been a mere mistake in the printing shop, but we looked into the matter a little more carefully, and so discovered the counterfeiting.

"Mr. Woodring is of especial interest to us in the Treasury. Possibly you may not know that our experts are skilled in recognizing the work of a counterfeiter. No matter how good he is, somehow he leaves his own mark on his work. If it is a known operator, we can usually tell the identity of the counterfeiter merely by examining his work. Unfortunately, not all these persons are in prison. Some of them have served their sentences. Some of them, though we were certain of their guilt, could not be convicted in court due to a lack of evidence. Some of them, though they have never actually counterfeited before, are skilled enough to do so, and we are on the watch for them. We want to know where all these persons are. But Mr. Woodring is a new operator. His work was unfamiliar to our experts."

"I understood he'd been in prison before."

"Yes, but not for counterfeiting. His offense was embezzling, and I believe there was a matter of some forged signatures involved. You can see the possibility of a connection. From forging signatures to forging engravers' plates is not such a very great step. Many criminals have made the jump."

"Mr. Woodring took a picture of a painting owned by Mr. Smith on a farm near here," said Ted suddenly. "Would that have been of help to him?"

"You do get around, don't you, Ted?" said Mr. Dunfield with a touch of admiration. "You understand that I'm not supposed to tell you anything more than necessary. There's nothing personal in that—it's just our manner of working. But yes, I know all about Mr. Smith's painting, and photographing the painting would have been a big help to Mr. Woodring. Let me explain it this way. Mr. Woodring wanted to copy the Blue Harvest stamps. Now why couldn't he simply have taken one of the genuine stamps and copied it? Well, he could, if he had to, but there are some decided technical disadvantages in working this way. These Blue Harvest stamps, even though genuine, would have small imperfections. By the time Mr. Woodring copied them, he would have added his own imperfections, and further faults might occur in the printing process. The final results might have been very poor.

"A counterfeiter likes to work on a large scale, and then have his work reduced in size. In this way any small errors he may have made will be minimized. Now he could have taken a genuine stamp and enlarged it—but this would have enlarged its imperfections as well, and wouldn't have been a great deal of help to him. These stamps were originally copied from a large painting. If Mr. Woodring could secure a copy of that same painting, and work from it, his results would probably be much better. And that, as you know, is what he did."

There was a pause. Mr. Dunfield had said that he wasn't supposed to tell more than necessary, and Ted knew that there had been some purpose behind this whole conversation. And he would have been less than astute had he not already guessed what that purpose was.

"Well, how about it, Ted?" asked Mr. Dunfield.

Ted knew what the Treasury man meant. He was asking if Ted had any idea where Mr. Woodring could be found. With some reluctance, Ted told about the cabin between the two waterfalls.

"I never heard of it," said the visitor, shaking his head. "Did he say it was in this state?"

"I kind of thought it was, but I—I guess he didn't actually say so."

Mr. Dunfield got to his feet. "Well, Ted, I think you've been of some help. If you should think of anything more to help me, here's my card, and you can call me collect at that number. And I don't think you should blame yourself at all over this affair. After all, there were a good many older, more experienced people who were taken in. Oh, yes, Ted. It would be of help to me if you'd be careful that nothing said in this conversation goes beyond this house."

Ted nodded.

"Good night, Mrs. Wilford," Mr. Dunfield called, as Mrs. Wilford appeared in the kitchen doorway. They showed their visitor out.

After the front door closed, Ted explained the situation briefly to his mother. She had known something about it before, but was more indignant than ever that Mr. Woodring should have involved her son in an affair of this kind. However, she couldn't see that it was Ted's fault, or that there was anything he could do about it.

"Maybe there is," said Ted, pondering. He got up suddenly, and going over to the telephone dialed Nelson's number. His friend finally came on.

"What's the matter, Ted?" asked Nelson sleepily. "House burn down or something?" He acted as though he was too tired to care very much, although Ted knew it was unusual for his friend to retire this early.

"I've been thinking about this Mr. Woodring matter—"

"Good for you!" said Nelson with some sarcasm. "I like people who think."

"No, seriously, I think I gave up too soon."

"What do you mean? You just got finished telling me that it didn't make any difference if we caught Mr. Woodring or not."

"I know, but I didn't think the thing through. If he gets away with it this time, how do we know he won't try the same thing somewhere else?"

"How can he?" said Nelson indifferently. "He can't pass off counterfeit Blue Harvest stamps unless he's working for the Blue Harvest company. And they won't hire him again. Anyway, I shouldn't think they would. I know I wouldn't—"

"Why does it have to be Blue Harvest? I've heard there are about three hundred stamp companies in the country." He was being very careful not to mention the possibility of counterfeit currency, still keeping in mind his promise to Mr. Dunfield.

"Keep talking. I know you're going to ask a favor of me, but I'm not sure yet what it is. Do you expect me to find a town that disappeared, or twin waterfalls that no one ever heard of, or—"

"No, nothing like that. I'm after something I know we can find. When Mr. Woodring came out here, he was accompanied by another salesman—I don't know his name, but he works out of Johnston City. Maybe he could tell us something about Mr. Woodring."

CHAPTER 14

A CYNICAL PERSON

Early the next morning Ted and Nelson were in Johnston City, across the state line. It had been a fairly long drive, and Ted had insisted they get an early start.

"I want to try to catch him before he gets out on his rounds," he had explained.

They did not know the salesman's name, nor was Blue Harvest listed in the telephone book. But a call to information speedily got them the number. Ted dialed the office and explained his mission.

"All right, if you can get it over with inside of fifteen minutes," the salesman told him. He didn't sound particularly friendly or unfriendly, but simply in a hurry.

"Can do," Ted assured him, and within a few minutes he and Nelson had presented themselves at the office, a small place just off Main Street.

Mr. Harridge, they learned, was alone in the office. Either he did not have a secretary, or else the secretary had not yet come in.

The callers introduced themselves, and Mr. Harridge invited them to sit down. Ted had taken a quick glance around, and he saw that the place was very similar to the Blue Harvest office in Forestdale. Large posters advertised the plan, and some of the premiums were displayed in the window.

"I suppose you've heard about Mr. Woodring," Ted began.

"Yes and no," Mr. Harridge returned. "That is, I received a very peculiar call from the home office Tuesday morning. They didn't tell me very much, but I could easily see that something was in the wind. Putting two and two together, I've got a pretty good idea of what happened."

"What about those purple-cow stamps?" Nelson questioned. "Did you get some of them, too?"

For answer, Mr. Harridge went over to the desk and took out a book of stamps and opened them. There could be no question but that these were a perfect blue. They were the first really blue stamps Nelson had seen, but Ted remembered seeing the same kind that first day at the *Town Crier* office. Even Nelson was now sure there was a difference.

"Then you didn't get stung with these purple stamps?" he asked discerningly.

"No, mine are all perfectly good. It wouldn't have been possible for anyone to pawn any of these counterfeit stamps off on me, anyway. Mr. Woodring and I each received our carton of stamps at the home office, sealed up. We were told not to check them with the baggage, and so we didn't, but kept them with us in our compartment. The seal on my box was still intact when I arrived here, and so, I presume, was Mr. Woodring's. He must have substituted the counterfeit stamps later."

"Then what's he going to do with his good stamps?"

"Oh, he can always dispose of them at a profit. It's getting the counterfeit stamps into circulation that's the problem."

Ted took up the questioning. "Did you know Mr. Woodring very well—I mean, apart from just coming out here with him?"

"Oh, I knew him in a business way, talked with him, had lunch with him, if that's what you mean. I didn't know anything about his personal life. I don't think he has any relatives, or even any settled home."

"Did you know that he'd been in prison?"

The man hesitated before he finally said:

"All right, I'll play it level with you, though I'd just as soon you didn't repeat this to anyone. Yes, I did know he'd been in prison. I met Mr. Woodring in some casual business way—I forget just how. Anyway, we got to talking. He was unemployed at the time, and looking for work. I didn't think that should be much of a problem with him, since sales jobs were fairly easy to find. But when he got a little more confidential, he told me what his problem was. He just didn't think he could land much of a job if an employer knew about his prison record. It happened that he'd had a couple of unfortunate experiences along that line. Oh, he could get jobs, of a sort, but people were always suspicious of him—didn't quite trust him—and he felt he could never get ahead that way.

"I asked him how long ago he'd been in prison, and he said ten years. Good heavens, ten years ago! If a man's managed to go straight for ten years, I should think that ought to be long enough for people to forget everything that happened before that. Besides, he'd been quite young at the time, and you can always hold out more hope for a young person who's gone wrong.

"I told Mr. Woodring that Blue Harvest was looking for salesmen, and that I knew as a matter of company policy they didn't check back references for more than five years. When he heard that, he decided to give it a try, and the Blue Harvest company hired him. Of course, I told him he'd have to have some sort of story ready about where he *did* work ten years ago, just in case somebody asked him, but I knew that the company wouldn't check on it. Funny thing, I would have given you ten-to-one odds that Mr. Woodring would never get off the track again—but it just goes to show you."

His tone sounded exceedingly bitter. They were unable to tell whether it was owing to his disappointment in human nature, or whether he felt his prestige with the company had slipped because of having recommended Mr. Woodring.

"Oh, this Blue Harvest outfit is all right, but It's a young, new company," Mr. Harridge went on, "and it's made a lot of mistakes. Not checking references properly is just one of them. I could tell you some others. They don't pay their salesmen enough. Oh, they give good bonuses for selling new customers, and that's why I've stayed with them so far. But after you've pretty well covered your territory, you know you aren't going to get very many new customers after that. It becomes mostly a matter of keeping the old customers serviced and satisfied. But without those bonuses coming in, the salesmen will all soon drift off, and the company will find itself high and dry. I could tell them, but they wouldn't listen to me. They'll find out in time. I won't be around very much longer myself."

Ted didn't think it either a very loyal or a very wise policy for a man to criticize his employer, especially to strangers. But Mr. Harridge went on:

"I can tell you another thing they're doing wrong: those premiums. What sort of items make the best premiums? It's things that people want, but would probably never buy for themselves. By allowing them to purchase premiums with stamps, you give them the feeling that they're getting them for nothing. What you're really doing is getting them to buy things they wouldn't otherwise buy, because they're a little bit too much of a luxury. Now toys don't come into that class at all. People will *always* buy toys, if they've got the money—you probably know that from your own parents. This puts us too much in competition with the regular stores."

Ted wasn't quite sure he followed this reasoning. It seemed to him that if customers were in the market for toys, then toys would make the best possible premiums. He wondered if Mr. Harridge wasn't being just a little bit *too* worldly, *too* all-knowing, *too* cynical.

"And you want to know something else that's wrong?" Mr. Harridge had apparently forgotten that he was in a hurry.

"'Blue Harvest' is wrong; I mean the name of the stamps. It sounds too countrified. Rural people don't want to be reminded that they live in the sticks. They want to pretend they're doing things just the way people in the big cities do them. If it were up to me, I'd change the name—make it Blue something else, and I wouldn't have a shock of corn on the stamps, you can bet your last dollar."

To Ted, the Blue Harvest stamps looked very attractive, and he didn't believe that all rural people were ashamed of living in the country and spent most of their time envying city people. However, he didn't see any point in arguing the matter, though he found it a little difficult to disguise his growing distaste for Mr. Harridge.

"Well, I don't suppose you can do anything about helping us find Mr. Woodring?" he asked.

"No, not a thing that I know of. Mr. Woodring never talked much about himself. As far as I'm concerned, I hope I never see him again. He talked me into recommending him one time, but he'll never get me to do anything more for him. Once burned, you know." He laughed.

Ted rose to go, and Nelson followed his lead. "Well, thanks anyway," Ted offered.

"Oh, sure." Mr. Harridge called after them, as Ted was about to open the door, "Say, do you know somebody named Ken Kutler?"

"Yes, I do," Ted admitted, turning partly around. "What about him?"

"Oh, not much, except that he was here yesterday, asking me most of those same questions. Claimed to be a newspaper reporter."

"He is," Ted assured him, and they went outside.

"Ken's always right there in the middle of whatever's happening, isn't he?" said Nelson, shaking his head.

"Yes, if he isn't breathing down your neck he's out there a step ahead of you."

"Think there's a story in this, Ted?"

"Must be—or anyway Ken thinks so. Well, as far as I'm concerned it's all between Carl and Ken. Carl wouldn't let me help him on it, even if I wanted to."

"No, and you don't want to—not any more than I want a double-scoop chocolate malted right this minute. How about it?"

"You're on!"

They stopped at a drugstore, and were soon sipping away at their favorite drink. At last Ted said thoughtfully:

"What did you think of Mr. Harridge?"

"Him? Oh, why bother about him? You can see exactly the kind of guy he is. He's one of those slick salesmen who can put on his best company manners, slap you on the back, tell the latest stories, and all that sort of thing. Only we weren't customers, and so he didn't have to put on his act for us. We saw him the way he really is. I think there's something insincere about all salesmen."

"Oh, I wouldn't say that. It's true they have to keep cheerful and smiling, whether they feel like it or not, and pretend the customer's always right, even when they'd like to give him a good kick in the pants. But *everybody* has to do the same thing, sometime or other. After all, you don't tell company to go home, just because it's past your bedtime. I guess salesmen have their troubles, like everyone else. Mr. Harridge is just an example of the kind I don't like."

"I like sincere people," Nelson maintained.

"Oh, he was *sincere,* all right, especially when he told us everything that was wrong with the Blue Harvest company. I think he meant every word of it."

"I guess we had our trip out here for nothing, didn't we?" asked Nelson, sipping happily.

"Oh, mostly, unless you call it important *not* finding out something—I suppose it sometimes is. We picked up a few little things, though. For instance, Mr. Woodring was the only salesman who had the counterfeit stamps. Of course that's what we thought all along. Well, I guess that about ends it. I couldn't do anything more even if—" He bit his lip sharply. He was about to mention his promise to the Treasury man to do what he could to help find Mr. Woodring, but fortunately caught himself in time. "I guess I might as well spend my time looking for Nancy's lost town."

"You seeing Nancy pretty steadily?"

"Oh, yes. She and Miss Monroe are coming to dinner tonight. I wish I could do something to help Nancy, but she doesn't seem to know very much about Freeport. She said there's a waterfall—"

Suddenly Ted caught himself. "A waterfall! Say, we're already looking for a waterfall, or a twin waterfall. I wonder if they could be the same?"

"Sure," Nelson agreed sarcastically. "Nancy lost a town—you can't find it. A waterfall is missing—you can't find it. That means they must be lost together. It sounds like good logic to me."

This cooled Ted off a little, but he wasn't quite ready to give up his idea. "Well, I don't know. Remember, there aren't very many waterfalls in this state. It couldn't be a very *big* waterfall, or we'd have heard about it. It just could be that there's something else special about it. Maybe it *was* a twin waterfall near Freeport, the same twin waterfall we're looking for now."

"The main thing about this waterfall," Nelson remarked, "is that it disappears every time anyone tries to find it. Do you think it swallowed up the whole town of Freeport?"

Ted didn't know exactly what he did think, except that the idea that the waterfalls were connected intrigued him. Sometimes someone puts two such ideas together, without very much reason to do so. Ted realized this, and while he proposed to be cautious about the whole thing, he still hoped the opportunity might come up to test out his idea.

"I wonder just where Freeport could have been anyway?" he mused.

"Port," Nelson pointed out. "That must mean water."

"Yes, and if it's in this state, it's not on the coast, so that must mean a lake or a river. Well, which is it?"

"I don't think it could be a lake," Nelson decided. "None of our lakes are large enough to be called really navigable—just large enough for pleasure boats. Oh, I suppose there'd be nothing to stop a town from calling itself a port, even if it was only on a shallow lake. But a river sounds more likely to me. Some of our rivers are navigable—for smaller ships, that is."

"Yes, but suppose it is a river, which one can it be?"

"If Nancy's and Mr. Woodring's waterfalls are the same, it must be north. That was the way Mr. Woodring indicated. But his car was found south of here."

"All the more reason to think he went in any direction *but* south. Well, even if it is north, that doesn't quite pinpoint it down. I wonder what we can do now?"

"How about taking a motor trip up every river, and seeing if we can find a town they forgot to put on the maps?"

Ted shook his head. "That's always the problem. Why isn't the town on the maps, and how could it disappear? I don't know, but I'm afraid we're not going to find it—not until we have a little more to go on than we do now."

"You still set on finding Mr. Woodring, Ted? After all, it might be pretty difficult to prosecute him, as long as Mr. Bentley refuses to cooperate."

"I know that. I wonder if Mr. Smith could help out there? If he could identify Mr. Woodring as the man who took that picture, it should link Mr. Woodring to the crime, even without Mr. Bentley's help."

"But do you think Mr. Smith could identify him? He sounded awfully vague about it to me."

"I know—a left-handed young man wearing a raincoat. I don't suppose that's the kind of evidence which would hold up in court."

Ted sighed, and placing some coins on the counter, they left the drugstore.

CHAPTER 15

THE PEOPLE'S VOICE

Ted and his mother enjoyed a pleasant dinner and evening with their visitors. During the evening Ted found a chance to ask Nancy once more about Freeport and the waterfall.

"Was there anything unusual about this waterfall, Nancy?" he inquired. "Did your grandmother say anything particular about it in her letters?"

Nancy tried to recollect. "Nothing very special that I remember, Ted. She described it as being very pretty, without being particularly spectacular." She frowned for a moment. "I recall one puzzling thing. She mentioned taking a visitor out for a ride to see the waterfall—I suppose she meant with a horse and buggy—and on a different route back they saw the waterfall again. I suppose that's possible—but her second description didn't quite match the first. You would almost have thought it was a different waterfall."

Ted's heart leaped up. "Maybe it was a *twin* waterfall, Nancy. Do you think it could have been?"

"Well, I suppose it could be," she returned hesitantly. "Will that help us to find it?"

"No, I guess not," Ted was forced to admit. "But at least Mr. Woodring mentioned a twin waterfall, so it must exist somewhere. And if it exists, you'd think somebody would know about it."

Friday morning the *Town Crier* came out with its account of the Blue Harvest mix-up. The story was very much as Ted had expected. Mr. Bentley's statement concerning the genuineness of the stamps was given prominent mention, but the other side of the question was also covered. And, as Mr. Dobson had promised, there was a long article on an inside page discussing the trading-stamp situation. Quite a number of townspeople were asked to give their opinion of the stamps. In general the women tended to support the idea, while the men were less enthusiastic.

Ted went out to buy a copy of the North Ridge *News-Record,* and he found that Ken Kutler also had a story about the Blue Harvest stamps. The story was entitled boldly, "Is There a Purple Cow?" and Ken discussed the situation much more bluntly than Mr. Dobson. Although a statement from Mr. Bentley was also included, any reader of the *News-Record,* was going to get the idea that there was some skullduggery going on. However, both stories were very careful not to accuse Mr. Woodring of any criminal act, nor even an alleged criminal act. This was very necessary, since there was no warrant out for Mr. Woodring, nor had he been indicted.

When Ted got home and was able to read the *Town Crier* more carefully, he found another item to interest him. There was a column of letters to the editor, called *The People's Voice.* One of the letters came from Rideaway, a considerable distance from Forestdale. The letter discussed the painting by Jan Fountaine, called *A Study at Twilight,* but more popularly known as *The Purple Cow.*

Were the people of Forestdale aware, the letter asked, that the painting had been done very close to Forestdale? In fact, the artist had worked in a quaint building known as the Dutch Mill. If visitors to the mill would look out the south window on the second story, they would see the very same view which had so inspired the artist. The letter went on to tell something about the artist's life and some of his other work.

This letter was puzzling to Ted. Although the writer had not mentioned that this painting had been used on the Blue Harvest stamps, he must have known it. It was the Blue Harvest stamps which had inspired all this renewed interest in *The Purple Cow.* But how could the letter writer have known all that he did? Some of this information was not yet general knowledge. It seemed to Ted there were some people who knew a good deal more about what was going on than they were likely to admit.

The writer of this letter was of particular interest to Ted. He wondered, if the signature was genuine—very often signatures were not, especially coming from a distant town where it would be difficult to check. If Francis Masters, the name signed to the letter, was the name of a real person, Ted wished he might meet him, and perhaps learn all that he knew about this matter. If it was not a real name, then it offered all sorts of possibilities. In any case, the writer of the letter must have had a good reason for writing such a letter at that particular time.

There was an easy way to check it. Ted addressed a special-delivery letter to Mr. Masters. In it he asked some rather unimportant question about the painting. He didn't really expect any answer to the letter; he was more interested in seeing whether the letter was delivered at all. He could hardly expect to know before Monday, and on Monday, when the mailman came, he had his answer. His own letter was returned to him, stamped "No Such Address." That letter in the *Town Crier* had been clearly a plant.

Again he put through the inevitable call to Nelson. "How about taking a ride out to the Dutch Mill this morning?" he suggested.

"O.K. Anything special?"

"I don't know," said Ted briefly. "I'll tell you later."

Out at the mill they made their way in, and went upstairs to the south bedroom, the scene of their scare on the night of the hayride. By this time Ted had explained to Nelson about the letter, and Nelson looked out the window critically.

"What do you think, Ted?" he asked.

"I couldn't really say," said Ted doubtfully. "It's awfully hard to tell."

"I know. It isn't twilight, and there isn't any cow coming along a country lane. Even if there *was* a cow, the artist would have to imagine it as being a lot closer than it could have been really."

"Yes, that's the trouble. Artists use their imaginations so much that it's hard to say where reality leaves off and imagination begins. It *could* be that the artist painted *The Purple Cow* standing right here where we're standing now. There're several hills in the background, just as there are on the stamps. And there's a fence, even if there aren't any cornshocks. I'm confused." Ted shook his head rapidly.

"I don't get it, Ted. What difference does it make to us whether the artist painted the picture here or not? Oh, there might be a little bit of local glory about it, but I don't think it's going to help us find Mr. Woodring."

"I don't know what to think about it, Nel. All I'm sure of is that the writer of that letter in the *Town Crier* had some special purpose in drawing our attention to this room. But I don't know what it is. I don't see anything in here, do you?"

They looked around carefully, but the room was empty—very empty. There were no expected traces of debris. The Dutch family had been careful to leave everything in tiptop shape when it moved out. They left the room, and looked around through the other rooms upstairs, all of them empty. There was a ladder leading to a loft through a trapdoor in the ceiling. Ted climbed the ladder, pushed open the door, and stuck his head inside. Then he came down and shook his head once more.

"Nothing up there, except a lot of old cobwebs. It's just an old attic. But it looks like the squirrels *did* get in up there. I don't suppose the family ever went up there, except perhaps to adjust the blades when they needed fixing. Listen to them."

Once more the blades seemed to be straining in the slight breeze. It gave the whole dusty, deserted place an eerie feeling. This old mill, picturesque though it might be, could hardly be described as cozy. It was too big and empty, too far from everything, placed thousands of miles away from where it really belonged. The boys looked through the downstairs rooms, and then found a door leading to the basement. It wasn't a full basement, but a mere dugout where vegetables had probably been stored. Anyway, there was nothing there for them to see. They came up again in a few minutes, and stepped outside into the bright sunshine.

"Now what?" asked Nelson.

"I don't know," Ted mused. "Mr. Masters certainly went to an unnecessary lot of trouble in order to call attention to that upstairs room. I wonder what he expected us to find?"

"There wasn't anything there," Nelson reminded him.

"I know, but—Hey!" Ted suddenly pounded his hands together. "Remember that tramp? *He* was there."

"Sure he was," said Nelson practically, "but he's gone now. You didn't expect him to sleep there for a week, did you?"

"No, not that," said Ted excitedly. "What I mean is that he was there before us. Maybe *he* found whatever there was to find first, and took it with him."

"Found what?" asked Nelson skeptically.

"That's exactly what I'd like to know."

"Then what did that letter writer want us to come out here and find it for, if it's gone already?"

"How does he know it's gone? He may have planted it here weeks ago. He couldn't know that the tramp found it first."

"Well, maybe," said Nelson, scratching his head. "But if there *was* something here, and a tramp *did* take it, what good does it do us now? It's just as good as gone forever."

With this Ted could hardly help but agree. Still, he didn't like to quit if there was still a chance.

"Where do you suppose that tramp went, after we scared him out of here?" he asked.

"Where would any tramp go? To the railroad, of course."

"And then where?"

"Well," said Nelson with a laugh, "the tracks only go two ways, so I suppose he went either one way or the other."

"That's not hard to figure out. But how did he go? Hop a freight, or shanks' mare?"

"He couldn't have hopped a freight along here very well, could he? There's no freight yard around. He must have walked here, stopped at the mill for the night, and when we disturbed him, continued on to wherever he was going."

"And where was that?"

"To the nearest freight yard, probably. And by this time he might be a thousand miles away. It's almost time for the tramps to start moving south, anyway."

"Yes, I know," Ted mused. "But I'm not so sure it had to happen that way. There's a lot of comradeship among these tramps. They get to know each other, eat together, exchange information. I wonder if this tramp couldn't have been heading for a nearby hobo camp? If he did, even if he's gone by now, he may have left some traces."

"Sure, and just where is the nearest hobo camp?"

"I don't know, but I know somebody who would—Ken Kutler."

"O.K.," Nelson went on, "so you find out where the hobo camp is, and then what do you do? You think you can just go down there and poke around, and they'll tell you everything you want to know? From what I've heard, they're a pretty close-mouthed bunch."

"Well, we can handle that when we come to it. If we don't learn anything, what are we out?"

"I'm not certain," Nelson murmured, "but you sure do drag me to the darnedest places. Well, I've never visited a hobo camp before, and it might be interesting. Maybe I'll like it so well that I'll *never* come back. When do you want to call Ken?"

"At the next drugstore."

"That'll be a quarter. Wait till we reach the other side of Forest-dale and you can call for a dime."

Ted smiled. Nelson had some rather peculiar ideas of economy and would actually have circled out of their way in order to save a little on the call.

"We're on this side, remember? There's a place. Let me off."

A few minutes later Ted returned to the car. "He knew where it was, all right. A place called Hoboville, and it's along the tracks, about ten miles down. What do you say we take a run down there tomorrow morning? Don't wear your best clothes—and don't bother to shave."

"Don't worry about me," Nelson agreed. "I'm not due for another shave for five days yet."

"Good. Oh, yes. Ken said one thing more: 'Say hello to the professor for me,' and then he laughed and hung up before I could ask him about it. I wonder what he meant?"

CHAPTER 16

THE SEARCH FOR THE PROFESSOR

"It should be along here." Nelson consulted his road map. "The fellow at the station said it wouldn't be on the map, but here's the ravine he told us about."

"That looks like a dirt road, coming up ahead," Ted observed, "just beyond that line of trees. Did he say how far down the road the camp is?"

"About a mile. This road goes to an old stone quarry, but he said you can't miss the camp. Kind of a dense underbrush, with a lot of little shacks scattered through there. He was kind of curious what we were going there for, but I didn't tell him anything."

"That's good—since you didn't have much to tell him anyway. Just that we're looking for a mysterious professor, and what a professor is doing in a place like that I wouldn't know."

"They must just call him that," was Nelson's opinion. "Well, here's the road. Hold on!"

This last advice was good, for the dirt road was heavily rutted and Nelson was obliged to reduce his speed considerably. They had not gone far before they saw a man trudging along, going in the same direction they were.

"Want to offer him a lift?" asked Nelson.

"Why?"

"Why not? He might be able to give us a little information. Anyway, it won't hurt to have a friend in this place."

While this man wasn't the sort of passenger they would ordinarily pick up on the open road, they reasoned that since they were heading into the hobo camp anyway, if one man was dangerous, then the whole idea of visiting the camp was crazy.

Nelson drew up a little ahead of the stranger and called out, "Want a ride, mister?"

The man looked up and smiled. He was a young man, not the older, tough, hobo type they had expected to find. His clothing was rough, and he certainly hadn't shaved for several days, but he looked quite intelligent.

"Sure," he agreed. "Sometimes it's that last mile that gets you."

He climbed in beside them. There was no need for either to ask the other where he was going, since there was only one place for the road to go.

"Nice weather," he remarked, as though to ward off any questions about himself.

They knew better than to ask any personal questions, but thought they might be able to get away with some general ones, such as "Where can we find the professor?" They Were going to have to start asking that question soon, and there seemed no better time to begin.

"Do you know someone called the 'professor'?" asked Ted.

"The 'professor'?" His manner became more guarded. "I know lots of professors—or I did once."

He was clearly going to be difficult. "No, I meant a professor out at the hobo camp."

"A professor in Hoboville?" the tramp countered blankly. "What would a professor be doing in a place like that?"

This was a question they couldn't answer, and wouldn't have felt like answering even if they could.

"Of course we don't know whether he's a *real* professor," explained Ted patiently. "It may be just a nickname."

"Lots of fellows have nicknames," the tramp mumbled. "Fact is, nearly everybody out there's got a nickname of some kind. They don't care much about telling their real names. It isn't that they've got anything to hide; they just want people to let them alone. That's why they took up hoboing in the first place."

He spoke of hoboing as though it were quite a respectable and normal occupation. Meanwhile, Ted realized, he had skillfully diverted them from their questions concerning the professor. Ted was determined not to be outwitted.

"A camp like this one—Hoboville, you called it—doesn't it usually have a person in charge?"

Their passenger looked vague. "I wouldn't know about that. Everybody's on the move pretty much. Maybe there's one fellow stays around more than the others; maybe there isn't. I never paid much attention to that, and I don't think you ought to, either."

In spite of their slow speed they were nearing the hobo village. If they didn't get some information out of him before they got there, Ted felt they never would. But how could they appeal to him to tell them what they wanted to know?

"Draw up on the side a minute, Nel," Ted suggested. Ted turned to the tramp once more. "Look, we're not tied up with the police or anything like that. We're just out for a little information, and we think maybe the professor could help us."

"What kind of information?" asked the tramp quickly.

"Well, it's kind of hard to explain. We think a certain tramp may have picked up a package—by mistake—and we'd like to know what it contained."

"If you don't know what was in it, what business is it of yours?" the tramp queried.

"Well, we *think* it's our business," Ted explained, "but if it turns out that it isn't, then that's all right, too. Somebody left a package for us to pick up, and by the time we got there it was gone."

"Then why don't you ask that somebody?" the man suggested.

"We can't very well. We don't know who it was." The explanation was becoming more involved, and it looked as though they weren't going to find out anything. There was no use explaining to the tramp they weren't even sure there *was* a package.

"You say you don't know who left the package, or what was in it, and you aren't sure whose package it is. Maybe the guy who found it has as much right to it as you have."

"That's right, he may," Ted agreed. "In that case he can keep it."

"He can keep it? Looks like he's got it already. Say, do you birds know any newspapermen?"

"Well, a couple," Ted admitted, "but we're not here for a newspaper story."

The tramp shook his head. "Newspapermen are almost as bad as cops. You know what I think? You look like two nice fellows, coming from good homes and everything. I think the best thing you could do is forget about all this, turn around, and go straight home. You might be fooling around with something you don't understand."

"Can't you just tell us if there is somebody called the 'professor'?" asked Ted.

"If there was somebody named the 'professor,' and you were supposed to know who he was, then you'd know. If you don't know, it's because you aren't supposed to know. I'm new here, and I'm not going to stick my neck out. But I still say you'd better go home. You won't get anywhere around here asking questions. Nobody'll tell you anything."

"Well, we'll try it, anyway," Ted said with a sigh, and Nelson started up the car again.

They could see the end of the road up ahead, and wondered if they had missed the village altogether, when their passenger told them to stop.

"Right here. Thanks for the lift. You can come up to my shack for a minute, if you want to."

They didn't see any shack, and partly out of curiosity they followed their strange passenger. He led them down a narrow, hardly marked woodland path, made a couple of turns at unexpected points, and presently they almost stumbled upon a rude lean-to, cleverly concealed among the underbrush.

"All the comforts of home," Nelson muttered sarcastically, for the shack certainly wasn't much to look at. Its materials were of the poorest sort, its workmanship crude. Still, to somebody it was home, and probably a big improvement over sleeping out in the cold and wet. It had a stovepipe sticking out the roof and a bucket of water with a dipper outside the door.

When they followed the man inside, they found a rough fireplace where the simplest kind of cooking was possible, a table, and a stool, and something that vaguely resembled a bed. For all its lack of elegance, it wasn't the worst place in the world, and they could imagine that even in the dead of winter a person might hole up here and be quite snug.

"Is this yours?" asked Ted.

"In a sense, yes. I just pulled in yesterday. It's mine for as long as I want it. Then I'll be on my way, and somebody else will use it."

Once more they couldn't avoid the feeling that there was some directing hand guiding the affairs of this encampment, but their host had refused to answer their questions about the professor, and they didn't know where else to turn for information.

"Well, I guess we'll stroll along," said Ted, after a few minutes. "I don't see anyone else around. Think we could find a couple of other residents if we scouted through this brush?"

"If you don't see them, it's because you aren't supposed to," the tramp warned. "I'd advise you to be on your way. However—" He shrugged, to show that he was going to accept no responsibility for what they did next. Maybe that was the whole trouble with these fellows, Ted thought—they didn't want to be responsible for anything.

After leaving the hut, they started down another trail. They followed the most unlikely turns, until presently they came upon another shack, very similar to the one they had just left.

"Must have had the same contractor," Nelson joked in a low voice.

At first they thought there was no one at home, but upon hearing them, a grizzled old man came out and motioned them to be on their way. Ted started to speak, but the man shook his head and continued his motions. Making one more futile attempt, Ted finally decided it was useless, and the boys retreated along the path.

"I guess our friend was right," Ted remarked. "Nobody's going to tell us anything. Well, it was a good idea, while it lasted."

"This is getting screwy," Nelson remarked. "First we were looking for a lost town; then a waterfall people can't locate; next a package that may not exist; and now it looks like we're hunting for a mythical man."

"Oh, he exists all right," said Ted with conviction. "Ken said so, and Ken knows. But he's about the most elusive character since Kilroy. Well, I don't see any help for it. Off we go, no wiser than when we came."

They returned to the car and drove off slowly. Twenty minutes later, when they were several miles along the main highway, Nelson chanced to ask Ted for the road map, lying on the seat beside him. When Ted reached for it, he gave an exclamation and held up a grimy wallet.

"Something our friend must have dropped. Think it's all right to look in it?"

"Sure. Why not? You always look in a wallet you find, to see if you can find who it belongs to."

While it was true they knew to whom this wallet belonged, they didn't know his name. Ted unfolded the wallet. There was no identification inside of any sort, nor was there any money in the bill compartment. At first Ted thought it was entirely empty, but upon exploring one of the pockets more fully he shook out a piece of metal—probably a lucky piece—and a little clump of hair followed. The hair was blond and curly—probably a girlfriend's.

"There's sometimes a secret compartment in those wallets," Nelson reminded his friend.

"I know. I'm looking for it." It took only a few moments more for Ted to discover the secret of the hidden compartment. He opened it and whistled. "Hey, pull over and take a look at this!"

Nelson did, and whistled, too. "Holy mackerel! How much is in there?"

"Over three hundred dollars. I never saw a hundred-dollar bill before—and I don't see very many of these fifties, either."

"That's some load of money for a tramp to be carrying around. I always *thought* some of those guys weren't as poor as they tried to pretend. Do you think he stole it?"

"Can't say. Maybe not. As far as we know it's his own money, and it's up to us to return it to him. You can't blame him for not flashing money like that around. He probably travels in some pretty questionable company. Well, let's turn around and head back. I've got a feeling somebody's going to be very, very happy to see us."

"You can say that again," Nelson agreed, as he turned the car around and headed them back toward Hoboville.

CHAPTER 17

A NIGHT IN HOBOVILLE

Their hobo friend was indeed glad to see them. He was looking very disturbed until he noticed their approach. Then he greeted them with a smile.

"Find it?" he asked. "I wasn't sure exactly where I dropped it, but I figured it was probably in the car."

"Yes, we found it," Nelson assured him, and handed the wallet over.

"Well, I'm surely glad to get *that* back," said the tramp in relief. He held up the lucky piece. "I got that from my mother. I can't say it's brought me very much good luck so far, but then, who can tell? Maybe I would have had a lot worse luck without it."

Apparently no one was going to say anything about the money in the secret compartment. The boys weren't going to mention it, and the tramp evidently was hopeful they hadn't found it. A certain anxious air betrayed the fact that he was eager to get off by himself for a moment to check the wallet.

"Is that lock of hair your mother's, too?" asked Nelson, with a thin touch of sarcasm.

"No, not my mother's. There was a girl—I cannot say her name. Somehow it just won't pass my lips. We were to be married on the first of June. The arrangements were made, the guests invited. Then, on the very last evening, there came a ring at the door. I answered it, and it was a message from—from her. She said she was going to marry another, a banker's son."

After telling his story as if it were the plot for an old-fashioned farce, he excused himself for a moment, and went inside the shack. When he came out again, he was in much better spirits.

"Oh, well," he concluded, "maybe it was all for the best. I surely do appreciate that you went to the trouble of returning my wallet, when there was nothing intrinsically valuable in it. Most young people would never have bothered. I guess I had you fellows sized up properly before—good character, fine, upright homes. I wish I could do something for you in return."

"Maybe you can," said Ted promptly, jumping at the chance. "You can tell us where to find the professor."

Their friend looked very thoughtful. Evidently he did feel that he owed them something; or possibly he might have been worried that they knew about the money and might tell.

"I wish I could get you to forget it, but I see that you won't. As I told you before, I'm rather new around here, and I don't want to exceed the bounds of the hospitality extended to me. But maybe I just might take a chance. Let me make it plain to you that there's no possible way for you to find the professor. Things aren't done in that fashion around here, and if they were it would be the worse for you. The only thing to be done is to let the professor find *you.*"

"How do we do that?" questioned Nelson with interest.

"Are you game to spend the night here in my place?"

The boys looked at each other. Neither was expected home for certain, so they knew the adventure was possible for them, if they cared to undertake it. But a night in a hobo town? "You're sure that's the only way?" asked Ted.

"I'm positive," said the tramp firmly.

"Then I guess we stay," Nelson agreed, with an air of resignation. "But won't it be kind of crowded?"

"Oh, I think the two of you can manage on the bunk. I'll find some other lodgings for the night."

It was still only the middle of the afternoon. The boys wandered around in the more open places, feeling sure their presence would not be welcome if they chanced to stumble upon some of the hidden shacks in the brush. Nor did they feel they could leave the spot. If they did—if they took the chance of calling home or sending any other messages—they felt somehow that this would be regarded as a suspicious circumstance, and that their chance of meeting the professor would be considerably lessened. They did meet a few of the other inhabitants of the village, mostly on their way to the brook to fetch water, and found them by no means unfriendly.

As the afternoon waned, the boys returned to the shack, and their friend presently appeared.

"Grub in fifteen minutes," he announced, which was welcome news to them. For all they knew, they might have had to go hungry until morning.

With twilight near, a bonfire was lit in a clearing, and now a good many more of the inhabitants—whether newly arrived or not the boys did not know—put in their appearance. Everyone was to cook his own supper, but there was a general sharing and exchanging, too. Nor did the boys feel particularly out of place. Their presence there was accepted as normal. ("As though somebody had given his approval of us," Ted whispered.) No questions were asked of them, and they could have participated in the general talk if they chose.

Soon bacon was sizzling in half-a-dozen frying pans, and the aroma was very appetizing. Their host also had a loaf of clean baker's bread, in a waxed wrapper. The boys decided to confine themselves to bacon sandwiches, which were very good, and they ate their fill. All around them the group of hoboes ate heartily, gobbling down their food with relish.

"I wonder if any of these fellows is the professor," Nelson murmured.

"Shh!" Ted cautioned him, fearing they might be overheard. He felt that it wasn't a wise thing to discuss the professor.

Ted and Nelson found there were three chief topics of conversation: criticisms of the government, sports, and "travel arrangements." This last was often a mystery to the boys, for the references were cryptic. Big Jake—evidently a railroad detective—was spoken of as being unfriendly, and an inquirer was advised to take another route. Certain towns were mentioned as being best to avoid, offering the possibility of jail sentences to vagrants, but there were also numerous places where generous handouts for a hungry man were to be had. Few of these men appeared to live more than one meal ahead at a time. None of them gave an impression of being at all vicious. They seemed to have been battered about by life, and not quite had what it takes to fight back.

The sports talk was very much the same as that of any group of men or older boys—with one exception. The scores they mentioned were about a week old, and the boys easily guessed they were dependent upon chance papers picked up along the road rather than the radio.

Ted got a special kick out of the political talk. It appeared that these men had one genuine beef—they were indignant that the social-security program had not been extended to cover them. At first glance it seemed unreasonable to expect to benefit from a program to which they had never contributed. But as the discussion proceeded, Ted felt they had some small measure of justice on their side. It was unfair to say they had never worked, when, in one fashion or another, they all managed to support themselves—which is, of course, the principal goal of work.

"The trouble is," Ted whispered to Nelson, "nobody would be able to tell for sure when one of these fellows retired. It would be hard to notice the difference."

When night fell, the boys, with nothing better to do, retired to the shack. They lay down on the bunk, and made themselves as comfortable as they could on its lumpy surface. But it was far earlier than their normal bedtime, and they did not feel at all sleepy. There was a quiet hum of country night life about them. They felt as if they were alone, out in the middle of a wilderness.

"I wonder what makes men take up a life like this?" Ted speculated.

"One of them said he had to take up an outdoor life for his health."

"If he had to have an outdoor walking life, why didn't he get a job as a mail carrier? No, there has to be more to it than that. It looks to me like each of them is running away from some problem in his personal life."

"I often thought I'd like to travel," Nelson mused, "but I wouldn't call this travel. What would you see? A lot of railroad tracks, and some hobo hangouts, and the inside of a jail if you weren't lucky. No money, and not very much grub. Nature may be wonderful, but I don't think I could appreciate it while I was hungry."

"Oh, they've all got a quirk of some sort," Ted decided. "I suppose somehow their lives just got too complicated, and they tried to go back to a simpler kind of existence."

"If you ask me, their problems are mostly inside themselves. I wonder what the professor is like, whether he's something special or just like all the others?"

There could be no answer to that just then, and presently they fell asleep. They were awakened in the early morning by their host, who came hurrying into the shack with good news for them.

"It's all set, boys. The professor will see you in fifteen minutes!"

This really was good news, and they tumbled out.

"I guess the lid's off, so I can tell you a little bit about the professor," the tramp explained. "He really was a college professor, a very highly regarded man. He ran into some trouble with his wife, and she hit him with a huge alimony settlement. Since almost everything he earned went to his wife, he didn't see any sense in earning anything, and so he ended up out here. He's done a lot for the boys—this is one of the best-run hobo camps in the country—and I guess they'd miss him badly if he left. But I don't think he ever intends to leave. He's happy just doing what he's doing."

"Just what is that?" asked Nelson.

"Besides running the camp, he serves as a liaison man between these travelers and society. They often need a man like him to bail them out of trouble."

Then their guide left them.

They had slept in their clothes, except for their shoes and jackets, and when they picked up the latter, Nelson felt in the pocket where he had left his wallet, then took it out and examined it.

"Somebody's been in here!" he decided.

"Anything missing?" asked Ted, reaching for his own wallet which he had also kept in his jacket.

"No, I guess not. Money's all there. Well, whoever it was, I hope he got some satisfaction out of examining my driver's license, hospitalization card, and a picture of my dog!"

Ted, too, thought that his own wallet had come under someone's scrutiny, for the various cards and memos he carried didn't appear to be in quite the same order he had left them. Nothing had been taken, however. Neither one made a habit of carrying very much money. Ted liked to have enough so that he could stop at a hotel and pay his bus fare home, in case he got stranded somewhere overnight, and Nelson carried a little extra, bearing in mind the possibility of repairs to his car. But the money they carried had proved no attraction to the intruder.

"I didn't hear anyone, did you?" asked Ted.

"No, but I slept like a log. I don't think anything short of a Number-Eight earthquake would have waked me up."

When they went to the car to get some things, they found that though the doors were locked, and the keys had never left Nelson's pocket, it was evident that someone had been in the car. They examined the glove compartment and side pockets along with the rear trunk.

"They're pretty thorough around here," Nelson muttered. "This is like being in a den of thieves—except that they didn't take anything. But they could easily have walked off with the whole works if they'd wanted to."

"They do look like they've had some experience," Ted agreed.

In a few minutes they joined their tramp friend again, and he led the way to the professor's house. The path they took was devious, winding about where no path seemed to exist, and it ended at a little plateau on a hillside, where it would have seemed no plateau existed. They would surely never have found the place by themselves.

The shack in which the professor lived was a little grander than the others, though it was far from a palace. Most incongruous of all, a flag fluttered from a pole.

As soon as they reached the clearing, their friend left them, and they approached the shack alone. They were uncertain whether they ought to knock or not, but just as Ted raised his hand to do so, a voice called out to them:

"Come in, boys, come in."

They entered, and found a quite comfortable living space. There was a fire roaring in the fireplace, the remains of a meal upon the table, the bed neatly made up, and most surprising of all, a large shelf of books. A rug had been spread upon the bare earthen floor.

The professor proved to be a gray-haired elderly man, erect and neat. His clothes were clean and pressed. He held out his hand and greeted them warmly.

"Hello, Ted. Hello, Nelson. I understand that you were both graduated from high school last spring, and are waiting to enter college. That's rather a crucial and exciting time of life—I've seen many young men just about to start out. You've each a good background to help you out. You'll find, Nelson, that your athletic endeavors will have valuable results in other fields. And Ted, you ought to go far.

Some of your work on the town newspaper has already attracted considerable attention."

"If you knew all this about us," said Nelson, flabbergasted, "why wouldn't you see us last night?"

"Ah, but I didn't know it last night. Won't you sit down?"

The chairs looked a little bit rickety, but they took a chance and sat down gingerly. The professor caught Ted's glance toward the bookshelf.

"Oh, my friends keep me well supplied with reading material. I need it for research on my book."

"Are you writing a book about hobo life?" asked Ted.

"No, nothing like that. It's a very dry treatise, I'm afraid, but it may prove of some value to persons working in its field. I trust you spent a pleasant night?"

The boys agreed that they had, but did not mention their nocturnal visitor, being sure the professor knew all about that.

"I have been informed of the purpose of your visit here," the professor began. "It touches upon a point over which we have a good deal of concern. It is our best intention to preserve the peace of our small, happy community by avoiding any possible clash with the denizens of the law. As you are probably aware, we here are in technical violation of the vagrancy laws—very unfair laws, I may state. I have serious doubts that the Supreme Court would uphold them, but unfortunately we've never had the funds to support a test case.

"However, we have reached a kind of tacit agreement with the police. They are not very anxious to arrest our members, since it would simply mean supporting them for a few days at county expense, and then requesting them to move on. We on our part undertake not to break the law ourselves—overlooking the illegal vagrancy laws—or to harbor persons that do. That is why I am most concerned that you have apparently accused one of our associates of purloining a package from a place known as the Dutch Mill."

"Oh, we didn't really mean to accuse anyone," Ted explained hastily. "We just *thought* there was such a package, and that a tramp—I mean one of your associates—may have taken it. We saw him jumping from a window at the mill, but we aren't sure whether he took anything with him or not. We'd just like to know."

"I understand, Ted. I may say at once that as of this moment I do not know whether there is any truth in your charge. However, I shall certainly check into the matter and ascertain the facts. If you will leave your address with me, I shall see that you are informed of the outcome by letter, at the earliest possible moment."

Ted felt disappointed. He had had this kind of brush-off often enough before. People always *said* they would write, or call back, and usually that was the last you ever heard. If other people did that, what could you expect of a hobo? The professor must have understood, for he said:

"I told you, Ted, that I *would* write, and if I say it, then you may rely on it."

He sounded sincere about it. But whether he was or not, there was nothing Ted could do about it.

He wrote out his address on a slip of paper, although he felt fairly sure that their nighttime visitor had already secured it for the professor. But the pretenses had to be maintained, and he handed it over. This seemed to be the end of the conference, and they rose to go.

Then another thought flashed across Ted's mind, and he turned back. Among all this group of tramps or "associates," surely every nook and corner of the state must have been penetrated at some time or other. And if this professor knew everything that was going on, wasn't it likely he might know about every *place* as well? Mightn't he know the location of the missing waterfall? At least it wouldn't hurt to ask, and Ted couldn't think of any other authority who was more likely to know the answer.

"Professor, do you know any place where there's a twin waterfall?"

"A twin waterfall? Certainly not. No such place exists."

He nodded in dismissal, and thanking him, the boys took their departure.

CHAPTER 18

THE FLOATING TOWN

As the boys drove away from Hoboville, they wondered just what the professor would be able to do for them.

"He *said* he'd write," Ted emphasized, "and so I suppose there's nothing we can do until we see whether he does or not."

"But will he know for sure?" Nelson pondered. "He isn't exactly a king. Maybe even he doesn't know everything that's going on."

"Oh, I think he'll find out all right. I have an idea that he has a widespread, loose-knit organization, mostly operating by word of mouth. I'll bet the professor knows everything that's going on in that camp and other related camps. But I'm not sure he'll tell us. His chief concern is to protect the camp and his men, and he might tell us only as much as he thinks is good for us to know."

"You giving up on your waterfall yet?" asked Nelson.

"No, I'm not giving up," said Ted firmly. "Didn't you think it was kind of funny the way the professor answered my question? He didn't say he had never heard of it. He said definitely there is no such place. How could he be sure there wasn't any such place, unless he was familiar with every possible spot in the whole country? It sounded as if he knew exactly what I was referring to."

"You've got a funny mind, Ted. He said there definitely wasn't any such place, and that makes you think there *is* one."

"I guess that's about the size of it," Ted admitted. Nelson often had a way of making his ideas sound absurd, but Ted clung to them anyway, until he was able to put them to the test.

Then there came a few days of impatient waiting for the professor's letter. Finally it came, almost as soon as it could reasonably have been expected. It was another of those dreary, rainy days, and the ink on the envelope ran slightly as Ted brought it in from the mailbox. He opened it and read:

Dear Ted:

Having checked into the matter which we discussed a few days ago, I am now able to state that your surmise was quite correct. One of our associates did inadvertently possess himself of such a package, secreted at the place you mentioned. It is now our intention to return this package to you, with the expectation that you will see to it that it ultimately comes into the proper hands.

As you approach Fremont over Route 17 you will pass over a small culvert just before reaching the city limits. The package is concealed beneath the northern end of the culvert, on the eastern side, on a slight stone ledge.

I regret this rather circuitous method of procedure, but it seems best to allow this package to remain in its present place of concealment until you reach there, meanwhile giving our associate a few days to leave the state.

Faithfully,

Professor λ

The letter was executed with the most graceful penmanship, and lacking a return address, it was difficult to believe it had originated in Hoboville. Ted was unable to decipher the letter following the last word, and decided it must be a Greek letter.

Of course he called Nelson at once, and Nelson came over in spite of the downpour. Nelson read the letter through.

"What does he mean by 'inadvertently'?" he asked.

"I guess what he means is that the tramp stole it and found he couldn't use it, so now he's willing to return it."

"There's something I don't get, Ted. The professor talks like he wants you to return this package to the person it belongs to, but how are you going to know that? You think there's a signature or something on the package?"

"I don't know. It doesn't sound like it, or the professor could have had it returned directly. I think it has to do with what's in the package. After we know what it is, we'll know to whom we're supposed to give it."

"Well, when do we start?" Nelson demanded.

Ted grinned. "I was just wondering if you'd want to go in all this rain."

"Sure, why not? We'll be dry enough in the car. Anyway, my curiosity's up, and I want to get to that package before anyone else has a chance to."

Deciding they might be gone overnight, or even possibly for an extra day or two, depending on how difficult it was to find the package and what they were expected to do with the contents, Ted packed up a few things and left a note for his mother. They also stopped at Nelson's home while he picked up a few articles. Shortly afterward they were out on the highway, headed northeast toward Fremont.

Nelson drove with special care, but with the traffic so light they made almost as good time as they would have made in dry weather. The rain, however, showed no signs of letting up. This was no mere drizzle. It was beating down in a heavy tattoo, rattling on the car roof.

"Maybe we can outrun it," Nelson observed. "After all, it can't be raining like this everywhere—"

"Look at that dark sky up ahead," Ted replied. "If anything, it looks worse there. We're just beginning to get into the thick of things. See the water tearing along in those ditches?"

On each side of the road dark, muddy water was swirling along at terrific speed, taking along with it branches and other debris. For the first time Nelson began to look worried.

"You know something, Ted? This isn't just an ordinary summer storm. It's been going on for hours. We must have had at least an inch or two of rain since we started out. I'll bet there're flood conditions along the banks of some of the streams and rivers. There must be a terrific runoff."

They continued on their way just the same, but with an ever stronger feeling they might be approaching catastrophe. The streams they passed were swollen and lapping at their banks, and wouldn't be capable of containing very much more of this flow. Persons who lived on low ground near them were likely to find themselves in trouble.

Nelson switched on his car radio to get the latest news. The music was soon interrupted with a weather report, which said that flood conditions were expected to prevail in that section of the state. Motorists were advised to stay out of the area unless they had urgent business there.

"I wonder if that means us," said Ted who, much as he would have liked the adventure, had a natural prudence which sought to avoid unnecessary trouble, especially trouble that he might be causing other people.

"I suppose it does," Nelson agreed, "but we're not very far from Fremont now, and I hate to turn back. Besides, you might say that we do have urgent business there. That package sounds like it might be awfully important, and we can't take a chance on anything happening to it."

Somewhat reluctantly Ted gave his consent, and they continued onward. But the rain was still heavy, and the windshield wipers were barely able to keep ahead of the streams of water flowing down the glass, offering them a clouded picture of the road ahead. Nelson had reduced speed to half his usual pace. Water had collected at some of the low dips in the road, and as they rushed through a fine spray shot up all about them.

"Any chance of stalling the engine?" asked Ted.

"Sure there's a chance."

"What depth of water can you go through without stalling?"

"I don't know, but I don't know how deep the water is, either, so what difference does it make?" Nelson was beginning to feel gay. "We're in this now, and there's no way out."

Quite unexpectedly they came to a road sign announcing the limits of Fremont. Fremont, like many another community, must have posted its limits far beyond the inhabited area, for except for a few scattered buildings they were still in open country. There was no sign of the town up ahead, although their vision was severely restricted in any case.

"The outskirts of Fremont, and this is Route 17. We must have passed that culvert. What do you say we turn around and see if we can find it?"

Nelson obliged, and they retraced the road for a hundred yards or so.

"That must be it," Nelson shouted. "No wonder we didn't see it. The water's right up to the edge of the road. You couldn't even tell a culvert's there. Say, what do we do now, Ted? How are we going to get under the culvert with that water running so high?"

"Just at a guess, I'd say we *aren't* going to get to it—at least not right now. The only way to reach it would be with a skin-diving outfit, and I left mine home."

"Well, then, what do we do?" asked Nelson.

"Let's go on to Fremont. What else can we do? Maybe if we stay over for a day or two, the water'll let up, and we can get under that culvert."

"Well, O.K." Nelson turned the car around once more, and they headed toward Fremont. "I'll tell you what, though, Ted. I'm getting awfully worried about that package. The way that water's rushing, it might easily get carried away so we'll never find it. And even if it doesn't, we don't know what's in it. Maybe it's something perishable, and the water will destroy it before we have a chance to find it."

"Could be," said Ted philosophically, "but there's nothing we can do about it now. Maybe there'll be enough left of the package so we'll know what *was* in it, anyway. There'd better be," he added with a laugh, "for you'll never go to college with a mystery like that eating away at the back of your mind."

But it soon developed they could not reach the town of Fremont in their car. A larger, swollen stream cut off their approach to the town proper, though they could now make it out, lying on higher ground in the hills up ahead. There was no chance of dashing through *this* stream and hoping the engine wouldn't stall. Even Nelson had too much sense for that. The water was at least two feet deep, and possibly twice that. The stream ran alongside the road, so there was no bridge ordinarily needed, but the water was far above its usual level.

Nelson drew the car to a halt. "Well, what do we do now, Ted, wait? I wonder if it's possible to go forty days without starving."

"You can do what you like, but I'm not planning to sit here for forty days."

"Then what—wade?"

Ted looked dubiously at the water ahead. "It looks too deep for that. Maybe we can hire a rowboat somewhere around here. These farmers probably have boats to go out fishing on the river."

They were forced to take off their shoes and socks and roll up their trousers in order to leave the car and reach somewhat higher ground. Then they put on their shoes, and headed determinedly for the nearest house. The rain was still heavy, but they turned up their jacket collars and made the best of it. It wasn't such a bad deal, after all, and by the time they got home and told about it, it might almost seem like fun.

It was fortunate the farmer did have a rowboat, and was willing to rent it. He invited them inside to get dry, but they declined with thanks, saying they would soon get just as wet again. He brought out the boat and oars, and watched as they carried it down to the banks of the stream.

They had brought their luggage with them, so there was no need to return to the car. Nelson took his seat at the oars, while Ted shouted directions, and they headed across the stream in a long slant. Somewhere near the middle Ted suddenly cried:

"Look out! There's something floating there—looks like a kitten on a piece of wood. Let's see if we can't rescue it."

Following Ted's directions, Nelson maneuvered the boat close to the floating kitten. Ted reached down and scooped up the bedraggled cat and snuggled it close to his chest. Then he noticed the wood the kitten had been using as a raft, apparently a dislodged signpost. On it, painted in black characters, was the legend:

FREEPORT

"Freeport!" exclaimed Ted. "What do you know about that?"

"A town that didn't exist, and here the sign comes floating down to us on the river. You win, Ted. You must have been living right."

Only a small part of the mystery was explained, but Ted felt that the remainder would not long elude them. He managed to grab hold of the sign and tow it along with them. After all, this was the only tangible proof they had that Freeport had ever existed.

They drew up on the opposite bank. The suddenly-aroused kitten scrambled out of Ted's grasp and scooted off. Since it appeared to know exactly where it was going, they made no effort to pursue it. Ted looked at the sign once more, still unbelieving. No question about it, it really said Freeport.

As the farmer had instructed them, they drew the rowboat a safe distance up the embankment and overturned it, placing the oars beneath. This was the custom in the town, they had been told, and the farmers had never had any trouble with thieves or vandals. It would be safe enough there, until the farmer retrieved it. They started up toward Fremont, Ted still lugging the sign. They hailed a man they saw, busy salvaging lumber from the rising water.

Ted showed him the sign. "Ever hear of Freeport?" he asked.

"Of course I've heard of it," he returned with a grin.

"Well, where is it? It sounds like a town that dropped off the face of the earth."

"Where is it? Why, there it is." He motioned to the sign. "You're holding the whole town right in your hand."

"You mean *this* is Freeport?" asked Ted incredulously.

"Every bit of it. I've seen that sign many times before. Just a sign stuck out in the empty sand."

"But wasn't there a town of Freeport at one time?" Nelson interjected.

"As to that I couldn't very well say." The man looked rather vague. "To tell you the truth, I don't know very much about it. I'm kind of new around here. Tell you what, though, if you really want to know. Stop up to talk to Mr. Hubert Wiley. He's one of the oldest residents around here, and something of a historian as well. You'll find him about halfway up Park Street."

Thanking their informant, and reluctantly dropping the signpost which was really too heavy to carry, they headed uphill toward the town. They stopped a passer-by to ask further directions, and shortly arrived at the home of Mr. Wiley. He proved to be an elderly, cordial man, and invited them in even before they had a chance to state their business. Noticing how wet they were, he drew up chairs for them close to the blazing fire, and offered them a warm drink. Then he was ready to talk business.

"Is there really a town of Freeport?" Ted questioned. "We found a signpost, but we've never been able to find it on any map."

"Oh, yes, there is a Freeport—or at least there was. It was located down by the river. The only trouble with the location was the bad floods every few years. After one of the worst ones, the mayor of the town, a Mrs. Marybelle Lindell, led a movement to move the town to higher ground. There was a good deal of opposition. Some people thought that commerce would be ruined if they lost close contact with the river, and they favored petitioning the state legislature to build a dam. Mrs. Lindell said they ought to stop whining to the legislature and try to help themselves. She negotiated with a railroad to build a line up here, and with the railroad to depend on instead of the river, her move won favor. They moved the town lock, stock, and barrel. What they couldn't take with them, I guess the floods took care of. For many years there's been nothing left of Freeport except that sign. Of course Freeport wouldn't do for the name of the new town, so they called it Free-mountain, or Fremont."

"Did you know Mrs. Lindell?" Ted questioned. "We're acquainted with her granddaughter, and she's very anxious to learn something about her relative."

"Oh, yes, I knew Mrs. Lindell very well. I was a friend of hers—a much younger friend."

He rose and walked over to the bookcase, and returned with several volumes in his hand.

"Here are some of the diaries Mrs. Lindell kept. I'm sure her granddaughter would be interested in these, and if she's really a relative, she's more entitled to them than I. But I have a kind of historical library here which I am going to donate to the town. Perhaps, when she is finished with these, she might like to return them to me."

"I'm sure she will, Mr. Wiley," said Ted warmly. "You've been most helpful. Perhaps she would like to write to you, and you could tell her something more about her grandmother."

"I'd like that very much, son. I don't get much chance nowadays to reminisce about the old times."

"Is there a waterfall near here?" asked Ted. "There seems to be some question about that."

"Oh, yes, we have a very fine waterfall. Not as big as Niagara, or anything like that, but we local people are very proud of it."

"Is it a double waterfall, by any chance?"

"Yes, it's quite a unique twin waterfall. I'm sure you'll enjoy a chance to see it before you go home."

"But somebody who ought to know assured us that there was no such twin waterfall," Nelson objected.

"How long ago was that?"

"About three days."

Mr. Wiley chuckled. "Three days ago it didn't exist." He went on to explain, "We do have a waterfall, pretty, but just a regular, single waterfall. It is only on rare occasions, like a heavy thaw in spring or an exceptionally heavy downpour like this one, that the flow gets too heavy up above the waterfall, and part of the stream is diverted to make a second waterfall. That is when we're most proud of our waterfall. Unfortunately, we seldom get the chance to show it off to visitors, but photographs of it have been widely distributed."

So the mystery of the disappearing twin waterfall was as easily explained as the mystery of the disappearing town. They rose and thanked their host most sincerely for his help.

"This granddaughter," said Mr. Wiley, with his hand on the door, "what is she like?"

"Well—"

Ted was at a loss how to describe Nancy. "She's very attractive, and a nice personality."

"I'm sure she must be," the old man mused. "If you would care to take a message to her, tell her to try to be like her grandmother." He shook his head. "A remarkable woman. A most remarkable woman."

CHAPTER 19

WHOSE PRISONER?

The boys took a room at the hotel, and changed into dry clothes at last. There wasn't very much for them to do, except to sit out the storm. They talked awhile, went downstairs to eat, and came back to wait for some of their favorite television programs to come on. Outside, the rain was less torrential than before, but was still falling steadily.

"What'll we do till the water goes down and we can get under that culvert?" asked Nelson.

"Don't you remember?" said Ted grimly. "I've still got a hunch that we're going to find Mr. Woodring somewhere up in a cabin, between those two waterfalls."

"O.K., so we find him—then what will we do?"

"Talk things over. Maybe we can persuade him to go back to Forestdale."

"Go back to Forestdale!" Nelson wrinkled up his nose. "In the name of all common sense, why?"

"It might help to get a few loose ends straightened out. And he might be willing to help us out by filling in the details of this scheme of his."

"Sure, sure," said Nelson cynically, "and talk his way right into a jail cell."

"Oh, I don't think it'll come to that. Blue Harvest doesn't seem at all anxious to prosecute."

When morning came, the worst of the storm seemed to be over, though there was still a light drizzle falling. The boys decided not to let that deter them. The thought of sitting around a hotel room all day doing nothing wasn't very attractive to them. It would be much more fun to get outside and see what they could do about locating Mr. Woodring.

They had no trouble at all finding the first waterfall. Situated just beyond and above the town, it was a well-known landmark. The second waterfall could not be seen from where they stood, and they reasoned that it must be out of sight, around the other side of the hill.

Their first problem was to find a way of crossing the stream. A pool of water had collected below the waterfall, and they figured it was altogether too deep for them. Instead, they climbed above the falls, until they found a place where the clear water looked shallow enough for them to take a chance. Taking off their shoes and socks, they crossed in safely. Shod once more, they turned to a survey of the hillside.

"He said it was a spot from which he could see both waterfalls," Ted recollected. "That means it has to be right along here somewhere. What's our better bet, up or down?"

"Up," Nelson decided. "The way he described it, it was pretty isolated. Going down, you're getting too close to the town."

Ted more or less agreed, so they began to climb the hill, scanning the hillside while they kept warily alert for slippery spots along the path.

"Is that a wisp of smoke up there?" asked Ted, squinting into the sky.

"Can't tell," was Nelson's response, for the day was so heavily overcast it was difficult to determine. "It might be. Let's try it."

They were about to start off when a grim voice behind them brought them to a halt.

"That you, Ted? I might have known it wouldn't take you long to come nosing around. And I think I've seen this friend of yours before, too. Well, now that you've come this far, you might as well continue all the way. March straight ahead, and turn right by that big tree."

Turning about, they saw that the person addressing them was Mr. Woodring. His manner was stern and unfriendly. Silently they turned back on the path and started upward, following his directions. They felt a little chagrined about it all. They had hoped to find Mr. Woodring, but instead it looked as though he had found them. Whatever they had intended, Mr. Woodring appeared to hold the upper hand.

Arriving at the cabin, they pushed the door open and went inside. Mr. Woodring followed, and closed the door behind them. It was a cozy little place, well furnished and nicely kept up. For an outdoors man, it was an ideal retreat from the affairs of a busy world.

The boys took off their jackets and sat down. Although Mr. Woodring also removed his coat, he remained standing, his manner menacing.

"Well, Ted, it wasn't so hard to find me, was it? I remembered afterward that I let something slip to you, riding home that day from North Ridge, but I hoped you'd forgotten. It didn't do for me to underestimate you. But now that you're here, exactly what do you want?"

"I was hoping I could persuade you to come back to Forestdale," said Ted seriously. "There are some people there I know would like to talk with you."

"Who?" He laughed bitterly. "Some police officers?"

"No, not that I know of. There's no warrant out for your arrest."

"No warrant?" Mr. Woodring looked thoughtful. "You're sure about that, Ted?"

"At least there wasn't when we left town. Of course I can't promise you that there *won't* be, but maybe if you'd come back and talk things over everything could be worked out."

"What about Mr. Bentley? Have you talked to him?"

"Yes, I have, and he didn't seem at all anxious to prosecute. He felt the publicity might hurt the stamp plan."

"Of course he might change his mind—"

"I don't think so. When your car was found he had to make some explanations to the police, but he must have done all right. Nothing more came of it."

"Yes, I can see where Mr. Bentley might not be very anxious to prosecute." Mr. Woodring seemed to be turning the whole thing over in his mind. "Of course I'm just taking your word that there isn't any warrant, but somehow I believe you. And as long as I can stay out of jail, there are reasons why I would like to go back. Maybe that would be the best way out."

"Then you'll come?"

"Like this?" Mr. Woodring's hand went to his face, and Ted took it that he referred to his growth of beard, his rather straggly hair, and his unpressed clothes.

"I understood you had plenty of money with you," said Ted, almost questioningly.

"Money? Sure, checks, big ones. But if I'd left a trail of checks behind me, that would have been about the easiest way for someone to find me, wouldn't it?"

For answer Ted took out his wallet, found a ten-dollar bill, and placed it on the table. Mr. Woodring did not look at the money, nor did he make any effort to thank Ted.

"Then you will go back?"

"Might as well," said Mr. Woodring grudgingly. "Part of the money from these checks rightfully belongs to me, and if we can work out a settlement, I'll be able to collect my share. I don't dare try to cash them the way things stand right now."

"Then you'll let us go?" asked Nelson hopefully. "There isn't any point in keeping us prisoner here, as long as you're giving yourself up anyway."

"Who's keeping *who* prisoner? I thought you boys were keeping *me* prisoner." He laughed, and the boys were obliged to join in, for it was a queer situation.

"I guess we're agreed, then, that nobody is anybody's prisoner," Mr. Woodring went on. "Am I to drive back with you?"

"No, you'd better not wait for us," Ted advised him. "We're stuck here in town for a couple of days."

* * * *

"You just threw away your ten dollars," Nelson assured Ted when they got outside. "He'll never show up in town."

"Well, it was a gamble. Maybe he will. As he said, he's got some money due him, and he'd like to settle accounts. Maybe he's really sorry for everything, and would like to straighten it out if he can."

"*Sure,* he's sorry. They all are, after they're caught."

The rain ended finally. The boys visited the culvert several times, and toward the end of the second day the water had receded sufficiently so they were able to spot the ledge where the package was supposed to be. They probed deeply, and found that it was still there, stuffed way back in the shadows. The paper covering had been thoroughly soaked and torn, but the contents, heavy metal of some sort, seemed not to have suffered. Ted tore away the remainder of the wrappings and held up two plates of copper.

"Wow!" he remarked.

"What is it?" asked Nelson curiously.

"Engravers' plates. It looks like these were used to print those counterfeit trading stamps. I'm afraid this is bad news for Mr. Woodring."

"Why?" Nelson demanded.

"Because when the Treasury man sees these, there'll *have* to be a prosecution."

"The *which?"* Nelson exclaimed.

There was no help for it, Ted had really let the cat out of the bag this time. But it was an almost unavoidable slip, for it was foolish to try to hide part of the story from Nelson, when they had the evidence of the plates right there in their hands.

"So that's it," said Nelson, nodding his head. "I thought it was queer how at one time you were all for letting Mr. Woodring go, and later you were all for tracking him down. I didn't quite catch on, though. I guess I'm not as fast with my head as I am with my feet."

It was clear now to whom the plates should be turned over. The professor had intended that they should be delivered to the proper authorities, and Ted proposed to do so. The Treasury man would probably be more interested in these than would the local police, and Ted still had his number to call.

"Know something? Don't you think it's awfully queer that these plates just *happened* to be hidden near Fremont? I'll bet it didn't just happen. The professor wanted it to be that way. He wanted me to find my waterfall."

"How come? He didn't seem very anxious to tell you the other day. Also, how did the professor know where Mr. Woodring was hiding?"

"At first I think he was just being cautious. He didn't know then just what the significance of the waterfall was, so he decided to play it cagey. But my question about the waterfall must have started him thinking. I don't think he knew anything at all about the case until we called on him. Afterward he investigated quickly, learned how Mr. Woodring had disappeared, and discovered that he really was hiding up in his cabin. The professor then hid the plates near Fremont, insuring that I would find Mr. Woodring. He almost *had* to do that. If he'd gotten himself into the position of protecting a counterfeiter, he would have been in some *real* trouble. By turning Mr. Woodring in indirectly, instead of reporting him himself, he was hoping to avoid getting involved in the affair."

There was nothing further to keep the boys in Fremont, and they started out for Forestdale, arriving very late at night. Even so, Ted was up very early, and hurried down to the *Town Crier* office. After all, he still had loyalty and obligation to the paper, and there was every reason why they should have first crack at the story—particularly since Ted had a hunch that Ken Kutler wasn't very far behind on the trail.

He knew Mr. Dobson would be absent from the office this morning, and he would probably run into Carl Allison at about this time. But this time it was all right with Ted. He couldn't hope to avoid Carl forever, and anyway it would be up to Carl to write the story. Carl listened with a superior air while Ted outlined the whole case. When he had finished, Carl said:

"Honestly, Ted, do you think I'm stupid enough to use a story like that?"

"What do you mean?" asked Ted, his eyes narrowing. "I've got the evidence right here—these engravers' plates."

"Sure, you've got them. But how do I know where they came from? I haven't seen any evidence to link them with Mr. Woodring."

"Who else could they be linked with?"

"I don't know. You tell me."

"We know Mr. Woodring has a criminal record—"

"What about it? So have lots of men. That's not enough to convict them of a new crime."

"He lied about working for that company in Chicago—"

"Wouldn't you, too, if you had a past to live down? How else would you expect to get a chance to start over?"

"He told us the stamps paid 3 percent, when they paid only 2 percent."

"He didn't tell the merchants that, and they're the only ones who really matter."

"He took a photograph of that painting of Mr. Smith's."

"I haven't seen Mr. Smith identify him."

"He ran off with the company's car."

"He had a right to. They'd leased it to him."

Ted was growing more excited. "He also ran off with all the company's checks—"

"—and didn't cash them. Really, Ted, you'd better get something down in writing before you expect me to stick my neck out."

This was the way it always was with Carl. He'd find an objection to everything Ted tried to propose, and in the end it would come to an explosion. Carl was prepared for it now, but instead Ted began to smile.

"Thanks, Carl. You could be right," and he dashed out of the office, leaving a very puzzled reporter behind him.

At the hotel Ted found Mr. Woodring still held a room there, and he dashed up the stairs without waiting for the elevator. He knocked on Mr. Woodring's door, and it was opened promptly.

"Oh, Ted. I suppose you've come for your ten dollars. I'm sorry that I don't have it yet. Mr. Bentley is going to reach a settlement with me this afternoon, and I'll see that you get it then."

"No, I didn't come about the money. May I come in?" He pushed his way inside before Mr. Woodring could object, and sat down.

Mr. Woodring began to move about the room, gathering various things together. "Really, Ted, what do you want? I'm awfully busy just now, and frankly I'd just as soon be alone."

Very quietly Ted answered, "Why didn't you tell us that you were innocent, Mr. Woodring?"

The older man looked up slowly. "What makes you think I'm innocent?"

"It had to be that way," Ted explained. "It was too foolish a scheme to begin with, because the evidence would point directly to you. There wasn't any way you could profit very much—not as much as your job and your place in the community were worth. So I've been trying to think, all the way over here, how I could prove you didn't do it. Then I remembered that Mr. Smith said the man who came to take a photograph of *The Purple Cow* was left-handed. You wear your wrist watch on your left arm, and I've been watching you just now. You're right-handed, aren't you?"

Mr. Woodring stared at him, but said nothing.

"But why didn't you tell us?" Ted pleaded with him. "None of us wanted to condemn a man unheard."

"Because I didn't want to beg and plead with people who were unwilling to believe me," said Mr. Woodring bitterly. "Because I thought I was entitled to a belief in my basic integrity, just the way every man is. Apparently it never occurred to you before that I might be innocent. I talked to Mr. Dobson, and it hadn't occurred to him. I talked to Mr. Bentley, and it hadn't occurred to him. It seems that the thought never even crossed anyone's mind."

"No," Ted was forced to admit, "but there was one person—a reporter on the *Town Crier.* Maybe he was just trying to be difficult, but he showed me how we could all be wrong. Would it help now if I said 'I'm sorry'?"

"Yes, Ted, it would help. It always helps."

"Still, it wasn't *all* our fault, Mr. Woodring. You *did* do quite a few suspicious things. You lied to us a few times, and you *did* run away."

"If you're trying to tell me I've acted like a dope, you don't have to, Ted. I've told myself all that before. My trouble is that I'm suspicious of everybody—but remember it was people that made me that way. I've had people too suspicious of me in the past, and because they always suspected me, I came to suspect them. I always thought people *would* suspect me, every chance they got."

"You did slip once," Ted reminded him.

"Yes, and I thought I'd paid for it. Oh, that was such a dumb kid's stunt. Everybody else seemed to be grabbing everything they could get, and not caring very much how they went about it. I thought I'd make my pile, too. The scheme looked foolproof to me, but I can see now that I was almost certain to get caught. But it's not just a question of getting caught any more. That's not important. It's a question of doing what you know is right and decent and won't tear your insides apart."

"If you'd only told us," Ted reminded him.

"I wasn't sure I could prove it, even if I tried. From that first moment when you mentioned purple-cow stamps, and I looked at them and saw they were different from my samples—we usually deliver our stamps in sealed packages to our customers, you know—I felt the

Blue Harvest company had set me up as some kind of fall guy. Who would take my word against theirs?"

Ted shook his head. "No, the company is perfectly honest. There wouldn't have been any point giving you counterfeit stamps, when they had to redeem them anyway. It had to be someone else—"

Mr. Woodring nodded his head slowly. "I see that now. It had to be that man who came out on the train with me, Mr. Harridge. He was the only one who could have exchanged the boxes in our compartment on the train. I remember now he knew of my criminal record when he recommended me to the company. I guess he wanted someone around with a record like mine, to hold the bag when things got too hot for him. I remember something else, too. He told me it was all right to tell people the stamps paid 3 percent instead of two— not the merchants, of course, who would know what they were paying for the stamps, but the consumers. They'd never stop to count the stamps, and wouldn't know how to calculate it anyway. I only tried it once—I was new and felt almost desperate about putting the plan over, and I thought Mr. Harridge knew the ropes better than I. I soon saw that that was a mistake. You've got to put things over on an honest basis, if you want to get people to stick with you."

"Mr. Harridge worked pretty hard to pin the blame on you. He gave your first name to Mr. Smith. And he planted those plates in the Dutch Mill, then drew attention to them through that letter to the *Town Crier*. With the plates found near Forestdale, it would help to fasten the blame more firmly on you and assure a prosecution. I suppose he only did that at the end—when he was afraid of getting caught up with himself."

"I wonder what his plan was, anyway?" Mr. Woodring meditated.

"I've talked with a man from the Treasury, and he thinks this was just a preliminary experiment to a scheme for counterfeiting currency. He was sort of getting his hand in. Of course he could have picked up some money by selling the counterfeit stamps to merchants and pocketing the payments. I think that's what he intended, but when the stamps accidentally came out purple, the best he could do was palm them off on you. He could then sell your *good* stamps. Somebody has suggested that he may have been well paid besides, to cast public doubt on the Blue Harvest stamps, but that's something we won't know unless he tells us. Maybe none of this would have paid him a great deal, but it could be that the money was very important to him right now—he needed it to launch his counterfeiting plan."

"Well, Ted, I guess you've explained it pretty well. It does help a little to know I'm leaving behind at least one friend in this town."

"Oh, you'll have a lot more than *one*," Ted returned with a laugh. "You won't leave right away, will you, until after I've had a chance to talk with Mr. Dobson?"

CHAPTER 20

KEN'S VERDICT

When the next issue of the *Town Crier* came out there was a front-page editorial, headlined: "WELCOME BACK TO FOREST-DALE, MR. WOODRING." Mr. Dobson was not a man who hesitated to apologize when he knew himself to be at fault, and he had the resources to present an apology in the grandest manner. Mr. Woodring quickly had an offer of several jobs, but decided to stick with the Blue Harvest company after all.

"They gave me my first chance, Ted, and I feel a sense of loyalty toward them. And I have to thank you, too, Ted, for helping to straighten this thing out."

"I didn't do anything more than I ought to have done," Ted assured him, "after the things I almost did to hurt you."

"Well, we can forget all that now. I'm looking forward to years of service in Forestdale. I still like my cabin up in the hills, but I guess I'd grow tired of it if I were there all the time."

Even before the *Town Crier* came out, the police, working together with the Treasury man, Mr. Dunfield, had moved in for an arrest, and had caught Mr. Harridge before he could take alarm. It seemed certain that prosecution and conviction would follow.

Ted had one more person who felt grateful to him. Nancy came over, just before leaving town, to thank him for the diaries.

"They're wonderful, Ted. Mr. Wiley was right when he called my grandmother a remarkable woman. I'm going to copy these diaries completely, and then return them to Mr. Wiley as you promised. Someday, I think, someone may want to write a book about her. But best of all for me I feel that for the first time I'm getting acquainted with my family."

Ted walked out with her to the car, where Miss Monroe was waiting to drive her to the station.

"Good-by, Nancy. May I write to you while you're at college?"

"It would be awfully nice if you would, Ted. Aunt Marian will give you my address. Good-by, Ted. This summer has been fun."

One last call came for Ted, the night before he was to leave for two weeks with his brother in the city and then college. Ken Kutler called to offer his best wishes and his congratulations for Ted's work on the purple-cow story.

"Oh, I know you had your finger in that pie all right, Ted. It would only have been a few more days before I found Mr. Woodring myself, but you beat me to it. Well, I think this affair has had at least one lasting effect. The Blue Harvest company can try its darnedest, but from now on people around here won't call those stamps anything but Purple Cows."

"What did you think of Carl Allison's story about it?" asked Ted.

"As a matter of fact, Ted, I called him up to congratulate him about it. I noticed in particular that he didn't write about Mr. Woodring's past criminal record, or some of the mistakes he made—all things he could have put in if he'd wanted to be nasty."

"Mr. Dobson probably told him not to do that."

"Quite possibly, but Mr. Dobson didn't set the tone of the whole story. That showed the mark of a real newspaperman. I had my doubts about Allison before, but I can tell you right now: he'll do!"

www.ingramcontent.com/pod-product-compliance
Lightning Source LLC
Chambersburg PA
CBHW020651180626
46816CB00003B/1224

SONG TITLE SERIES

THE THREE CROONERS

FEATURING

MICHAEL BUBLÉ

HARRY CONNICK JR.

TONY BENNETT

JOAN MAGUIRE

Copyright Page

New: Three Crooners
Author: Joan Maguire

National Library of Australia Cataloguing-in-Publication – Publication entry

Creator:	Maguire, Joan author
Title:	Song title series: featuring Michael Bublé, Harry Connick Jr., Tony Bennett / Joan Maguire.
Edition	Large print edition
ISBN:	9780994329745 (paperback)
Series:	Song title series (large print); book 9.
Notes:	Includes bibliography references
Subjects	Bublé, Michael--Fiction.
	Connick, Harry, Jr., 1967---Fiction.
	Bennett, Tony, 1926---Fiction.
	Singers--Fiction
	Titles of musical compositions--Fiction
	Short stories, Australian

Dewey Number: A823.4
Published with the assistance of CreateSpace and is available through the Print On Demand Network or www.songtitleseries.com

The original short story book was created and written
By Joan Maguire on 1st August 2011 ©
ISBN: 978-0-9941998-0-5
E-book re-written April 2014©
EIBSN: 978-0-9925964-5-3
This book was converted into large print in March 2015 © and is available through the same distributors as the normal book or
www.songtitleseries.com
ISBN: 978-0-9943297-4-5 (large print)